Tourists

BOOKS BY RICHARD B. WRIGHT

Clara Callan
The Weekend Man
In the Middle of a Life
Farthing's Fortunes
Final Things
The Teacher's Daughter
Sunset Manor
The Age of Longing

Tourists

A NOVEL

Richard B. Wright

A Phyllis Bruce Book
Harper*Perennial*Canada
HarperCollins*Publishers*Ltd

Tourists

www.harpercanada.com

HarperCollins books may be purchased for educational, business, or sales promotional use. For information please write: Special Markets Department, HarperCollins Canada, 55 Avenue Road, Suite 2900, Toronto, Ontario, Canada M5R 3L2

First HarperPerennial Canada edition

National Library of Canada Cataloguing in Publication

Wright, Richard B., 1937–
Tourists / Richard B. Wright.

"A Phyllis Bruce Book".
ISBN 0-00-639240-7

I. Title.

PS8595.R6T68 2002 C813'.54
C2002-902413-7
PR9199.3.W7T6 2002

RRD 9 8 7 6 5 4 3 2 1

Printed and bound in the United States
Set in Sabon

For Kildare Dobbs

Know thyself!

The Oracle at Delphi

Know thyself! And be truly alarmed!

Philip Bannister

Tourists

One

Following my arrest at the airport, I asked whether Mexico still retained the death penalty, and if so, what particular form it assumed, whether hanging, shooting or garrotting. I have always held the view that people who live in hot climates are more bloodthirsty and vengeful than those of us who dwell in the temperate zones. The policeman, a grave-looking fellow, said nothing as he took my arm. Beside him were two other miniature men in blue uniforms. Although I am only five foot nine, I towered over my captors, for this was Cozumel, a green island off the Yucatán Peninsula, and the lawmen were descendants of the Maya, a people who once flourished in these parts despite their diminutive stature. Earlier in the week, in fact, I had remarked to my wife that the stolid brown little women in their long dresses and shawls looked as durable as chess pieces. I imagined that people with such a low centre of gravity would be very difficult to tip over in a scrap.

As they led me away, the little policemen spared me the indignity of manacles, and for this I was grateful. Other tourists, sitting in the departure lounge with their straw hats and souvenirs, regarded us with interest. They doubtless thought I had contravened some minor regulation under the Custom and Tariff Act.

On the way to the police station nothing was said, and

in this grim silence I stared out at the jungle that lined both sides of the road. Through the trees I glimpsed a tin roof gleaming in the late morning sunlight. It was very hot in the car. The policeman beside me also had nothing more remarkable to do than gaze out his window at the unprepossessing landscape of palmetto and scrub palm. Now and again he absently fingered his moustache, while I wondered how they had discovered the bodies. Had the robot salesman led them to the murder site? Will people never learn to mind their own business? The driver swerved around a straw-hatted man on a bicycle, while I reflected dismally on the enormous fuss that lay ahead of me. I can't abide disorder or confusion, but it was difficult to see how either could be avoided. There would be tedious conversations over the telephone. Things would have to be repeated for the benefit of my aunt's aged ears. *Joan's bed? Oh, dead! Good heavens, Philip, how did that happen? What dear, I can't hear you. You're where? In jail?? What on earth for?*

There would, of course, have to be funeral arrangements. I would have to see about getting Joan's body back to Canada. Or would that be done for me? And what of the Hackers? Surely someone would have to fly down and claim the remains (an ugly turn of phrase). It was an awful mess, really, and for what it's worth, may I say right now that I'm sorry I did it. I supposed, too, that I would have to get in touch with Ross Parry, a man I've disliked since our school years when he bullied me without mercy. Yet I knew my aunts would insist on it, for they stand by tradition, and the firm of Thrust and Parry has been my family's solicitors for probably a hundred years. Ross's grandfather and mine were classmates at

The Gannymede. Still, I couldn't imagine Ross being very sympathetic to my plight, nor could I see either him or Jack Thrust mounting an inspired defence; their business is conducted mostly in the drab coin of wills and estate planning. They would probably turn me over to someone who defends murderers for a living. The school would also have to be notified. Bea Corcoran and Clayton Clapper would cover my classes, but I was also scheduled to address the chapel on Monday morning. I had planned indeed to make notes for my talk "Both Ends of the Candle" on the flight home. My arrest, of course, put paid to that notion.

The boys enjoyed my homilies. I always try to insert a joke or two and afterward I am often congratulated on my sense of humour. I can't see that it does any harm to begin the school day with a smile. Neddy Blake is far too dry and Milo Murdoch is hopeless. And so it would fall upon the headmaster to speak in my absence. I guessed he would have the devil's own time explaining that I was in a Mexican jail, charged with the murder of my wife and two American tourists.

Two

Avenida Rafael Melgar was filled with tourists walking past souvenir shops and restaurants. Vendors pedalled their bicycle carts and sold ice cream and oranges to passersby. Looking out my window toward the ocean, I saw a cruise ship flying the tricolour.

Our driver pressed his horn several times as we moved around taxis and motor scooters. The police station was at the edge of town behind the Municipal Building. The policeman escorted me into a large room of bleak grey cement past several local people who were lined up in front of clerks; something to do with licences for motor scooters or payment for traffic violations. Someone opened a little gate, and we went behind a long counter to a door. One of the policemen knocked upon it.

From within came a command in Spanish and we entered. Behind the desk sat J. Humberto, or so a sign on his desk said. The uniformed policeman quickly withdrew. Looking up, Mr. Humberto appraised me briefly and waved toward a chair by his desk. "Sit," he ordered. He was a portly man in his middle years with a sad worried face.

While I sat, Mr. Humberto studied papers which doubtless had to do with my vile crime. The air conditioner was faulty, and now and then emitted a rasping sound; it seemed to be on its last legs and gave forth cool air only intermittently. As Mr. Humberto read, he shook his head as though disbelieving the words in front of him. Finally he looked across at me and said, "This is a very unwholesome situation, Señor Bannister. You have brought a major disgrace upon the island."

He turned aside to display a gloomy profile. Leaning his elbows on the sides of his chair he made a fat little tent with his hands, settling the apex against his chin. "We have always enjoyed such a good reputation," he said. "This is a wonderful place for tourists. Here they can relax and enjoy the splendours of the Caribbean." Mr. Humberto dismantled the little tent by opening his hands. "A variety of glass bottom boats provide a unique view of our colourful marine life. The best snorkelling and scuba diving in the world are minutes from your hotel door. After a day at the beach and following a pleasant meal at any of our various restaurants with their seafood specialties, visitors can stroll the streets of San Miguel in the mellow evening light. Sometimes the chords of a guitar can be heard softly playing from open doorways. Many of the hotels have mariachi bands and floor shows. There is also a cinema where tourists can catch a glimpse of authentic native life, for here the island's inhabitants like to relax in front of the pictures." Mr. Humberto stopped to give me a sidelong glance. "We try to put people at their ease, Señor Bannister. Hospitality is the name of the game. We do not have gangsters and drug addicts like Florida. A man can bring his wife and children down to Cozumel and know that they will not be beaten and robbed. And now you have seriously damaged our reputation. For that I can never forgive you."

"I am sorry," I said.

"Ha! Sorry!" exclaimed Mr. Humberto. "It is so easy to say, isn't it? So easy to say after the fact." He arose and walked to the air conditioner, which was now making only gasping noises. Mr. Humberto struck the appliance with the heel of his hand but nothing came of it. "Such things," he said, returning to his desk, "frighten away tourists. It is a well-known fact that murder is very bad for business. I will catch it from the merchants." He sat down and glared at me. "You do not have to be at the Chamber of Commerce dinner next Monday night. Oh no! You will be safely tucked away in your cell. It is I who will have to endure the slings and arrows." He paused and looked glumly at the papers on his desk. "You have complicated my life, Señor Bannister," he muttered, "and if I live to be a hundred years old I shall never forgive you. I swear on my mother's grave."

When the telephone rang he pursed his lips and sighed. There followed a torrent of Spanish. At first Mr. Humberto spoke, but then the receiver crackled. Mr. Humberto held it away from his ear and gazed at me with reproach in his eyes. Once he interrupted to say, "*No. No Americano. Un Canadiense. Sí! Sí!*" Mostly, however, he listened to his caller with a look of evident dismay.

It is chastening to hear strangers talking about you in a foreign tongue and in an ill humour. It made me wonder what civil rights, if any, I possessed. But whoever inquires into such matters before travelling to another country? One would almost certainly be considered neurotic for doing so. I guessed that one of the things to do would be to get in touch with the Canadian consulate. But where the devil would the nearest one be? To tell you the truth, I was more concerned about the effect of this news on my aunts. I could picture Ross Parry telling them in his blunt manner about my dilemma. While Mr. Humberto talked, I decided that Neddy Blake would have to tell my aunts. As school chaplain Neddy has had a good deal of experience in the conveyance of sad tidings: it is Neddy whom the headmaster calls upon when a father drops dead at a business conference or a mother runs off with her pottery class instructor.

I was thinking of Neddy and of how to get in touch with him, when Mr. Humberto hung up the telephone and stared at me. "This is all so extremely unpleasant, Señor Bannister," he said. "And so unnecessary." He got up and began to pace about the room with his hands in his trouser pockets. "It has always been my belief," he announced, "that murder is unnecessary. It is such a stupid way of dealing with a problem." He shook his head at the folly of it all. "And now to business," he said briskly. "Some people from Chetumal are on their way to see you. Chetumal is the state capital, for your information. They will take you back to the prison there in due course. They are very stern people, Señor Bannister. I have heard reports."

He returned to his chair and sat down with his hands still in his pockets. "For the unpleasantness you have caused they will no doubt beat the shit out of you. At least," he added, "I hope so. It goes without saying that I myself am too civilized to oversee such actions. But you will not always be so fortunate. Oh, no indeed! Over the next few weeks you can expect your share of tribulation and rightly so." He leaned forward. "It will go well for you if you tell me what happened before the others arrive with their truncheons and cattle prods. I want details, Señor Bannister. Details of the murders and the sexual orgies at the El Gringo Hotel. Lying, of course, will be futile. You will only dig yourself deeper into the soup, because we have a witness. An employee at the hotel saw one of your horrible orgies." Mr. Humberto pronounced *orgies* with a hard "g" as in *agriculture*.

The air conditioner began again to wheeze and Mr. Humberto looked suddenly mournful. "Murders and sexual orgies," he said. "Such things are not for holiday fun spots."

Three

Do not for a moment disbelieve the old wives' tale that murderers are frequently tormented by their dreams. We are, indeed. Last night in my little cell I dreamt of Joan and me in the company of Ted and Corky Hacker. Introductions were in order; victims meet your slayer. We were naked as we shook hands. Perhaps the dream was a warning that in time I will become completely unhinged by guilt.

The dream itself was a mockery of our first meeting with the Hackers in the dining room of the El Gringo Hotel. It was our first evening on the island, a Sunday. The tour guide, a lively fellow in a red jacket, had organized a "Hi Neighbour" party in the hotel lounge; everyone gathered to drink a free rum punch and hear about the island. The man in the red jacket stood on a chair near the bar and answered questions about the drinking water and the exchange rate. Upon my urging, Joan and I left early.

The dining room was empty except for a couple seated at a corner table. The man looked brawny in his open-throated tropical shirt but his face was boyishly friendly. Riding his head was a great shock of blond hair, a pompadour in fact. He grinned as the maître d' seated us at our table. At the time I remember thinking as I glanced across the room that the man with the blond pompadour looked exactly the sort of fellow I would avoid sitting next to on an airplane. The woman with him was pretty in a fresh, innocent way. Under the Orphan Annie hairstyle her face looked utterly guileless. I saw her as one of the innumerable young housewives who appear on television game shows shrieking with delight and pressing their cheeks as they win electric golf carts and holidays in Hawaii.

At first I paid them little heed, for Joan and I were in the midst of another argument. Or perhaps it was the same argument we'd been having since we'd left home. The points of disagreement were various but mostly centred on her infidelities and my numerous failings as a husband. You must bear in mind that these quarrels were never conducted *fortissimo*. Neither of us struck an attitude nor raved; instead we quietly said nasty things to one another. On that particular occasion, if memory serves, Joan accused me yet again of being a snob. "Mr. Flintstone," she insisted, "is probably an absurdity, I grant you. But he was only being friendly in the manner of people on holiday. I've never understood why you cannot be more cordial at such events. You stand so apart, Philip. It's really quite off-putting. I shouldn't be surprised if we make no friends all week."

"Perhaps," I said, "but I do not relish being slapped on the back by a perfect stranger who is wearing white shoes. If it comes to that, I don't relish being slapped on the back by anyone."

"Oh fiddlesticks!" Joan said, lighting a cigarette. "You should loosen up. We're tourists in another country. You sound exactly like stuffy old Clifton Webb in *The Razor's Edge*. You even look like him in that blazer and school tie. You probably wish you had your ballsy old cricket team along, I shouldn't wonder."

Joan was Australian, but she had spent a great deal of time in England; indeed, she once married an Englishman (I was her third husband). During her residence in England, she unfortunately acquired some affected usage, including the frequent employment of the conditional tense: I should like, I should imagine, I shouldn't have thought, etc. Perfectly grammatical, of course, but this Winnie-the-Pooh English wore my nerves terribly.

"I don't remember," I said, "Clifton Webb in Maugham's novel."

Joan finished her margarita and smiled. "You know perfectly well that I'm referring to the film. Tyrone Power played the young man who forsook riches to seek life's meaning. I don't remember the girl who was in love with him. It was on the television a few weeks ago. A load of rubbish, actually. May I have another drink before we dine, lover?"

"I see no reason why not," I said, signalling for the waiter. "Moreover, I shall join you. Do you, by the way, know that couple across the room? They keep looking over here and smiling as if they know us."

Joan looked across and smiled at them. The man raised his glass. Turning to me, Joan said, "I've never seen them before in my life. But he's jolly good-looking, isn't he?"

"Are you asking my opinion of his appearance, foolish lady? I take no particular interest in whether men are good-looking or ill made."

"I'll bet," said Joan, looking at the couple again, "they're Americans. They look American to me."

"What I'm wondering," I said, "is whether the man is

quite in balance. He's been grinning at us ever since we walked into the room. For all we know, he could be a confidence man or an axe murderer."

Joan laughed and the braying sound filled the room. "My poor timid darling!"

"I am not timid," I said, "but it is unnerving to be persistently grinned at by a stranger. Surely even you would agree with that observation."

"My dear Philip," said Joan, leaning forward as though explaining simple matters to a child. "At resort hotels people are like members of a family. Friendships are quickly established. Informality reigns. You've led such a sheltered life in that funny old school."

I was prepared to deny that, but was interrupted by the waiter bearing our drinks. He also took our food order, while two other Mexicans in loose-fitting white smocks walked toward us. They looked like hospital orderlies but they had strapped guitars over their shoulders. They positioned themselves near our table.

"I'm very much afraid," I said, "that these people are going to sing to us."

"How wonderfully romantic!" said Joan, smiling at the musicians who had begun to strum and sing their nonsense. People were now drifting into the dining room. As he sang, one of the musicians gave Joan a sly grin.

Wherever Joan went she attracted males: policemen flirted with her as they wrote out speeding tickets, the dullness in old men's eyes vanished as she passed by them; I'm quite certain she figured prominently in the fantasies of the most priapic onanists in the school. It was not that she was beautiful; she had missed beauty by a fair margin. Her features were most irregular. Her teeth, for instance, were too large and slightly bucked. Her braying laughter suggested coarseness. But she was a large, handsome woman of forty years with a lively intelligent eye for the passing scene. And I think that what made her desirable was the air of merry lewdness she exuded. Behind her expensive clothes and affected English, Joan was really an Elizabethan tavern wench. Her powerful sensuality had once captured my heart and glands, and in the dining room of the El Gringo Hotel it worked its magic on the tiny musician as he plucked the strings of his instrument and sang in a sweet high voice. At the end of the song everyone applauded quietly, except for the man with the pompadour who clapped loudly for what seemed to me a very long time. The singers moved along to another table.

While we ate our dinner, the man and sometimes the woman would look over at us, and from time to time Joan smiled back at them. Exasperated I finally said, "I wish you'd stop flirting with that man. It's embarrassing." Joan finished the beer that had accompanied her meal.

"Don't be absurd, Philip. I'm not flirting with anyone. Besides, I've noticed you stealing a glance or two at the little lady. And she's certainly been staring at you. I rather think she fancies you, darling."

"Ridiculous," I said. Joan smiled. She was wearing a dirndl skirt and a low-cut peasant blouse that allowed her thick blonde hair to spill across her shoulders. I called this her Rita Hayworth look.

We had just started our coffee when the couple got up from their table and began to cross the room toward us. "Don't look now," said Joan, "but we are about to have visitors." In addition to his tropical shirt the man had dressed himself in checkered Bermuda shorts and lisle stockings. The woman wore a pale green pant suit.

"Good God in the sky above," I said.

"Now don't be snooty, my darling," said Joan. "This could be rather fun." There was an empty table next to ours and the man stood by it and smiled down at us.

"Hi there," he said.

"Hi there, yourself," said Joan.

"Mind if we sit down?" he asked.

"Why should we mind?" Joan said.

"You folks just get in today?"

"Yes," I said, "this afternoon."

"We've been here since Friday," said the woman.

"I think it's going to be a fun place," said the man. "We haven't had much of a chance to look around yet. My name's Hacker, by the way. Ted Hacker. And this is my wife, Caroline, though everyone calls her Corky. And believe you me she's a corker. She's had that name since she was a little girl, haven't you, hon bun? Cork's full of spunk and raring to go all the time." Hacker winked at me with a large blue eye.

We introduced ourselves and shook hands. Hacker's great fist was covered with fine blond hair. It may have been my imagination but I'm almost certain his wife tickled my palm as we shook hands. Joan appeared vastly amused by the Americans.

"It's very nice to meet you," she said.

"Say, I'll bet you're English," said Hacker.

"Well, not really," said Joan. "Actually, I'm Australian, though I haven't been back there in years." She lighted one of her long cigarettes.

"Still on the old cancer sticks, eh?" said Hacker. "Personally I gave them up cold turkey eight years ago on New Year's Eve. Haven't touched one since. And Corky has never smoked, have you, hon?"

"Only once," said Corky Hacker. "When I was about twelve. Behind our garage with a boy named Morley Sharples. Oh, we were both so sick!"

"Well, for Pete's sake, that doesn't count," said Hacker. "Why, that kind of experience is part of a normal American childhood. Smoking behind the garage is as normal as hot dogs at the ballpark. You can't count that as really smoking, Corky." He turned to us. "But say, I love to hear you people talk! Are you Australian too, Phil?"

"No," I said, "Canadian. So is my wife now, by citizenship."

"Well, all I can say about that," said Hacker, "is that you've got a great country up there. Some great fishing and hunting. A friend of mine goes up into Manitoba every fall, hunting for ducks and geese, though I'm personally opposed to the assassination of wildlife. Let the beasts of the field and the fowl of the air have a crack at life, too, is what I say." He paused to stroke a large smooth jaw that reminded me of a weapon.

"This your first time in old Mexico?"

"My first time," I said. "Joan's been here before."

Hacker looked narrowly at Joan. "Is that so? Stepped out on the old man, did you? Well, we've tried Florida and Arizona. California, of course. Thought we'd try something different this year. What line of work are you in, Phil?"

"I teach English in a private school," I said.

"Teacher, eh! Well, I've got a lot of respect for teachers. I'm in pharmaceuticals myself. Our company supplied the astronauts with all their pharmaceutical requirements. Free and gratis, of course. I need hardly add that it was a publicity venture." He looked suspiciously around the dining room and then said *sotto voce*, "Say, we were wondering if you folks would be interested in joining us for a postprandial libation. In a word, a drink. I make a mean margarita and I've got all the fixings in our room. What do you say?"

"It's kind of you, Mr. Hacker, but . . ."

Hacker abandoned his sinister whispering. "Call me Ted, Pill, phlease." He laughed abruptly. "I'll try that again if I may. Call me Ted, Phil, please. And listen, if coming up to our room doesn't grab you, what say we go into the local village and patronize a bistro? It's a beautiful evening."

"It sounds marvellous," said Joan.

"We'll see what the nightlife is like in old San Miguel. Isn't that the name of the burg, Cork?"

"I think so, Teddy."

"*Wunderbar*. It's only a couple of miles. We'll hail a cab. My treat. How do you like them apples, Phil?"

"Very nice apples," I said, "but I'm afraid I'm not up to it. Perhaps another time."

"Oh, Philip, do let's go," said Joan. "Let us be blithe and bonny."

"Sure," said Hacker, sitting back with his large hairy arms folded across his chest. "It's holiday time."

"Please come along," said Corky Hacker, smiling shyly at me.

"To tell you the truth," I said, "I'm not quite feeling up

to merriment. I have this rather bad headache." This was true; I did have a headache. "But," I continued, "why don't the three of you go ahead?"

Joan made a face at me. "Are you quite sure you wouldn't mind, darling?" It wouldn't have mattered if I had minded or not.

"Of course not," I said.

"Then it's settled," said Hacker, beaming at us. "Phil will trot off to bed with some aspirin while the three of us hit the town." He leaned forward and whispered, "How do you feel about group sex, Joanie?"

Joan's bark of laughter startled an elderly man at the next table, and Corky Hacker clapped a hand across her mouth to suppress a giggle. Hacker looked at me and again closed and opened a large blue eye. "A joke, Phil. Only a joke."

Four

Ted Hacker's mention of "group sex" struck me as peculiarly apposite insomuch as the phrase was included in the first sentence Joan ever uttered in my presence. This occurred over three years ago at a reception arranged by me for her second husband, the poet Dwight Tushy. As many of you know, Tushy was the author of such books as *Mrs. Donovan's Tiny Bird* and *Beast Music*. The latter, course, won the Governor General's Award and, because of the erotic nature of the verses, earned its author a measure of notoriety. At the behest of the headmaster at the time, Dr. Peach (now dead, alas), I arranged for Tushy to give a reading to the boys in Bung Hall. I was not enthusiastic about this event; I believed then and still do that Tushy was a literary charlatan. But the headmaster was insistent. The stubborn old man was due to retire the following spring and rumour had it that he planned to write his memoirs in verse. Over the past few months he had taken to wearing a black beret as he walked about the school grounds. He had seen Tushy on television promoting his latest volume, *I Love You, I Hate You, What Are You Going to Do about It?*

In his office Dr. Peach talked to me about *flair*. "The man has *flair*, Bannister, *flair*." He absently stroked the large mole on the top of his hairless head, something he always did when he was trying to appear reflective. As student and teacher I had seen him do it for over thirty years. Rubbing the mole became something of a joke around the school, as in "Watch Out! Peachy's at the mole again!" So in his office I watched him gaze out the window and stroke his mole. "Michaelmas," he said, "is a devilishly long term, as you well know, Bannister. The lads are listless. I sense *ennui* within the ranks. I can smell it. I sniff it in the classrooms and in the corridors. The old *taedium vitae*, Bannister. Acedia, the bane of any communal enterprise. It tainted monastic life throughout the Middle Ages. It is an enemy we must constantly be vigilant against. Forgive the preposition at the end of that sentence." He stopped rubbing. "I see this man Tushy as a tonic. A tonic that will see the lads through to the Christmas holidays. The faculty, too, will benefit. They have looked a little wan of late." His hand again explored the top of his head. "We'll have a little party for those of us interested in the arts. Sherry and water biscuits and Gentleman's Relish. Spare no expense. I imagine your apartment will do nicely for the occasion. Clapper and Corcoran will, of course, assist you, but as head of the department you must supervise matters. For reasons which escape me, he enjoys the experience of tending bar."

When I pointed out to the foolish old man that aside from being a bad poet, Tushy wrote verse that was perhaps inappropriate to our particular setting, Dr. Peach stopped rubbing his head and looked suddenly alert. With his head cocked to one side he resembled a large bird listening for a worm.

"Do you mean sex?" he said. "Oh piffle, Bannister. Forgive me, but *piffle* is the word that comes immediately to mind in the light of your objections. This is, after all, the last half of the twentieth century. Good heavens above, the sexual act cannot be ignored. Nor can the efforts of those artists who strive so valiantly to elucidate its meaning for all and sundry."

So Tushy, a large, menacing figure with a shaven head and wearing designer jeans and a plaid work shirt, came to The Gannymede. He read his dreadful verses in Bung Hall and the school was neither shocked nor intrigued. Only Bea Corcoran and Dr. Peach seemed inspired by the performance and applauded with spirit at its conclusion.

Afterward some of the faculty and their wives and a few selected students came to my apartment in Budger House. My aunts, who scrupulously attended every cultural event at the school, did not come in from the Land of Smiles Retirement Facility. As Aunt Flo said over the telephone, "Philip, your Aunt Fay and I have met some of the great poets of this century, including Max Bodenheim and Wystan Auden. We have no wish to mingle with the likes of Dwight Tushy." I could hardly blame them. In addition to being a bad poet, Tushy was an ill-natured and discourteous man. He quickly waved aside the sherry and in his famous gruff voice demanded spirits.

In my kitchen he quickly drank several ounces of my best malt whiskey.

"Has my goddamn wife arrived yet?" he asked.

I looked through the doorway at the small assembly in my living room. "I'm not sure, Mr. Tushy. I can't see from here."

The poet made an unpleasant farting sound with his lips. "*Mister* Tushy," he exclaimed. "Get off that crap. Call me Dwight. And find that fucking wife of mine. She was supposed to meet me here. The bitch never comes to my readings anymore." With his great naked head and in the work clothes, Tushy looked like an angry stevedore.

"What does she look like?" I asked. It was a meaningless question; his wife would surely be the only stranger in the room.

Tushy poured himself another tumbler of whiskey. "You probably couldn't miss the bitch in a snowstorm. Tall. Blonde. Probably her boobs will be hanging out of whatever she's wearing." Tushy looked suddenly morose as he waved his empty glass at the doorway. "Tell those people I'll join them in a few minutes. I have to prime myself for these shindigs."

While Tushy primed himself, I returned to the living room. Dr. Peach was standing near my harpsichord talking to Bea Corcoran. I prayed that the old man would keep his hands off the instrument. Clayton Clapper was serving canapés while infecting the surrounding air with his celebrated halitosis. I watched a young faculty wife grow pale as she accepted a cocktail sausage. The Neddy Blakes were conversing with some students from the Literary Society. Milo Murdoch, head of the science department and an enemy, was spilling pipe ash on my sofa as he talked to another of the young attractive wives. I have never understood why Murdoch appeared at these events; he knows nothing whatsoever about music or literature. Yet, you will always find him smirking about some recital in the chapel or at a speaking competition in Bung Hall. Watching him puff away on his vile pipe, I knew that I would later have to air the rooms.

In time Tushy was drunk enough to join us and, at Bea Corcoran's urging, he agreed to recite a few poems from

Beast Music. Among others, I remember his booming out two of his most famous and widely anthologized excrescences.

CRYING TOWEL HIS

You bought that kitten to annoy me.
It's glittering yellow eye
Reminds me
Of the navel I once kissed.
No more of that!
You can close your legs
For all I care.

CRYING TOWEL HERS

How dare you threaten
With the hanging flesh?
Its ugly snout
As purple as a bruise.
Those days are over
Big shot!

"'Purple as a bruise' is very good," murmured Polonius Peach. "A very apt figure of speech."

It was at this point that the tall woman with the slightly bucked teeth appeared by my side and whispered, "Do you approve of group sex?" She wore a long flowered dress and her large breasts were on display. Across the room Milo Murdoch took the pipe from his mouth and gaped, as the tall woman lay a hand against her throat and laughed. "I jest, of course," she said, offering me her hand. "I'm Joan Tushy, the great man's wife. Number four. And I shouldn't at all be surprised if you're not Philip Bannister, the host of this soiree."

She turned, a large forthright creature, and cast her shrewd and merry eyes over the room. "Has my dear husband been behaving himself?" She smiled at me. "What a lot of handsome young men you have about the place! Life in a boarding school must be hell if you're a homosexual." Joan Tushy studied me carefully. "I trust you're not a homosexual, Mr. Bannister?"

"I am not," I replied coldly.

In point of fact, most of the students and some of the faculty believed I was. This was a constant source of irritation to me. But then, most people nowadays believe that any bachelor over thirty is a homosexual, especially if he is interested in the arts and particular about order. I admit that I'm rather fussy, but what of it? It doesn't mean I relish the notion of someone's member inserted into my fundament.

Joan Tushy continued to appraise me. I have been accounted a handsome man, and over the years not a few women, often widows whose sons I have taught, have set their caps for me.

"You're not married, I know that," said Joan. I smiled mysteriously. "It's unusual," she said, "to meet a bachelor in his forties who isn't queer. What do you do for nooky in a place like this?"

"I manage," I said. She only looked amused, and I don't think she believed me.

The truth is that sex had never played a prominent role in my life. There always seemed so many other things to do; during term, life at The Gannymede was often hectic.

In my twenties I did have an affair with a plain quiet girl, a nurse named Lois Tunney. We met while I was in the hospital for minor surgery (inguinal hernia) and afterward became good friends. I would visit her apartment two or three times a month and we would listen to Chopin or Schubert. Then we had intercourse on her Axminster rug; she refused to use her bed and I never asked why. A few years ago Lois left for British Columbia to study theology. She is now an ordained minister in the United Church of Canada. We still exchange Christmas cards (Hi, Lois!).

My other intimate relationship involved a colleague. It was short-lived and had farcical overtones. Ten years ago Bea Corcoran arrived at The Gannymede. She was the first female teacher to be hired in the history of the school. It caused quite a stir among the older faculty members. But Bea was so engaging that she soon won over the doubters. She was fresh from university, a big, energetic, good-hearted girl with an undistinguished countenance.

At her first Christmas party she drank too liberally of Dr. Peach's eggnog and suggested we go to my apartment for a nightcap. As it happened, my aunts were then staying with me over the Christmas holidays, and so I suggested my office, where I always kept a bottle of vodka. Three or four times a year, when my nerves got the better of me, I drank a few ounces in the middle of the morning to fortify myself.

After Bea and I had a drink of vodka, a ludicrous scene developed. It was a particularly cold night, and beneath her outer garments Bea wore a kind of elaborate body stocking (she had purchased this the previous summer in

Norway, of all places). Since we were both a little the worse for drink, we had a sticky time getting her out of that. Then, being nicely settled on my couch, we were frozen into terrified silence by footsteps in the hallway. These belonged to old Gore, the watchman. He had obviously heard our scuffling about and so shone his flashlight through the frosted window of my door. Fortunately I had secured the lock, but the conscientious old man insisted on rattling the doorknob and calling out my name. He left only after I yelled out the news that I was thinking aloud in the dark. This doubtless confirmed old Gore's view that most of the faculty were madmen. After he left, Bea suggested we try again, but I was much too nervous to perform. We dressed without a word and left separately.

I suspect Bea has always held that evening against me, perhaps convincing herself that by rejecting her gifts I was making a personal statement. Women often get the oddest notions about sex. But, in any case, when she returned from the Christmas holidays Bea was cordial enough; we had both, it seems, decided to put the ridiculous event behind us and proceed with our lives. We remain good friends, and staunch allies at faculty meetings.

Standing next to Joan Tushy, I mulled over these little sexual adventures of mine before saying by way of conversation, "It must be interesting living with a poet?" The question was fatuous and, anyway, everyone knows the answer: life with a creative person is hell. The moods, my dear, etc.

Joan placed a hand on my arm and, leaning forward,

whispered, "Well, it's not very jolly for me, dear boy, because poor Dwight can't get it up anymore."

There was nothing to say to that. A stranger's sexual predicament is of no interest to me. But the woman seemed to be obsessed with matters sexual and that in itself was fascinating enough.

"All these dirty poems," continued Joan Tushy. "They're all fantasies."

Milo Murdoch was edging closer. His eyes were bulging at the sight of Joan's nearly naked bosom. "You're a handsome fellow, Philip Bannister," said Joan. "I expect other women have told you as much." I was prevented from making a suitably modest rejoinder by Neddy Blake, who beckoned urgently from across the room. He was already wearing his overcoat. The Blakes always left various functions early; it had something to do with Mrs. Neddy's kidneys. I knew Neddy wanted to discuss the use of the chapel for my forthcoming production of *Murder in the Cathedral.* We talked about this briefly and the Blakes left. To my dismay Dr. Peach began to play show tunes on my harpsichord. Behind the makeshift bar Captain Hale raised a tumbler of sherry and toasted me. He shouted something that was lost in the din. I suspect it had to do with the next cricket season; the Captain and I coached the first eleven. Now he looked bleary with drink. Tushy was surrounded by Bea Corcoran and members of the Literary Society.

The strangest thing then happened; I remember the moment quite clearly. I had opened one of the small leaded windows and was standing by it gazing out at the late November afternoon. It was nearly dark and it had been snowing for several hours. (Will I ever see snow again? I wonder.) Boys were shouting and throwing snowballs at one another as they walked to the dining room for supper. The chapel bell struck the hour. Soon my guests would leave and I would air the rooms and arrange for Mrs. Spinnaker to clean the apartment. Since it was Wednesday there would be a favourite meal of lamb hash and apricot fool in the dining hall. Later, several boys had appointments to see me regarding their academic fates. And so I stood by the open window, inhaling the fresh cold air and reading for perhaps the thousandth time The Gannymede's motto engraved along the archway near my window. *Auream quisquis mediocritatem Diligit*. And standing there I reflected on Horace's famous words and on the shapely disposition of my days. How pleasing it was to observe that order resided within the gates of that fine old school!

After a moment I abandoned this reverie and, looking back into my apartment, I found myself staring directly into Joan Tushy's roguish smile. Oh, I know it sounds absurdly romantic: strangers across the room, etc., etc. Why, fools have written songs about such unlikely occurrences. Yet it remains nevertheless true that from that very moment the order and symmetry of my life would be forever sundered. Ahead lay my own Scylla and Charybdis. I had fallen in love with the woman I was to marry and murder.

Five

Was I not cautioned about the unlikelihood of such a marriage proving successful? You may well ask; I was indeed, if only indirectly. After the announcement of our engagement, I became an object of interest and concern in the Common Room. Colleagues quietly congratulated me, but from time to time I would catch one of them peering at me with curiosity over the edge of his newspaper. Neddy Blake often shook his head wonderingly as he passed by me. Dr. Peach seems not to have been affected by the forthcoming event. Or perhaps he was not even aware of it, since more and more he remained in his office and worked on his memoirs. Only the boys seemed delighted by the news. As I heard one remark in the hallway, "Old Bannister isn't queer, after all! What do you know about that?"

My aunts were aghast at my choice of spouse. During our first visit they received Joan kindly but they were not amused. In the Sun Parlour of the Land of Smiles, Aunt Flo poured the tea and Aunt Fay passed the tray of biscuits. Each smiled gravely at Joan's little stories, which were often of a humorous nature. I had informed her of my aunts' interest in the arts and so Joan mentioned both her painting and her involvement in amateur theatre. It was an unsatisfactory interview.

Months later Bea Corcoran was to issue a more direct warning. At a small reception before our wedding, Bea, a little drunk and with the best will in the world, led me into a pantry behind the headmaster's summer kitchen. Even from there we could hear my future wife's great braying laughter. At the time it was music to my ears. In the tiny room Bea closed one eye, the better to bring my face into focus. "Philip," she asked. "Are you absolutely sure you know what you're doing?" But as Aunt Fay used to say of me as a child, "You can't change that boy's mind. Stubborn like his father. You might just as well save your breath to cool your porridge."

I anticipate, however, for at this point in the narrative Joan is still married to Dwight Tushy. Allow me then to sketch in the courtship that followed that afternoon in November over three years ago.

The end of term is always a busy time. I had to deal with *Murder in the Cathedral* and with Neddy, who fusses terribly when something of a secular nature is going on in his chapel. There were also examinations to mark and grades to prepare. Yet Joan Tushy was seldom far from my thoughts, and my smitten heart rejoiced when, some two weeks after my party, I received a letter from her thanking me for my hospitality. Uncharacteristically she admitted to being a bit fed up: her husband had descended into the severe melancholia that always followed the publication of one of his books, and the long and bleak Canadian winter lay ahead. To cheer herself up she had resumed an old pastime and enrolled in a painting course at the college of art. On Tuesday evenings she and her classmates sketched young naked men.

I wrote her a letter conveying the hope that her spirits would soon improve and touching on the pleasures and travails of life in my own small universe. I have always enjoyed writing and receiving letters; as a child I had several pen pals in outlandish places like Lahore and Mascara. My aunts encouraged me in this habit, believing that such exchanges of information promoted better understanding among races. Then at Christmas Joan sent me a homemade card: the silkscreen image of a kangaroo with its pouch filled with parcels. The lettering was charming and bore the words "'Tis the season for oysters what! Best Joan." Her reference to oysters sent me at once to my *Partridge's Dictionary of Historical Slang*, where indeed I discovered that the word *oysters* was an old euphemism for testicles. My merry Joan was her old self again.

A week later her husband killed himself. Some of you will recall reading about this grisly event in the newspapers. For those of you who didn't, but harbour a fascination for accounts of extreme behaviour, the following is what appears to have happened: the poet first drank a bottle of whiskey; then, in the darkness of the winter night he walked along the railway tracks near Hamilton, Ontario. Then, he lay down upon the tracks and allowed himself to be dismembered by a freight train. As Professor Doug Beamer of York University (his book on Tushy, *A Prairie Sinner*, was inflicted upon the public last year) told the newspaper people, Tushy's final act was in itself symbolic of the man and his work. Having grown up on the Canadian prairies, Tushy's verse is filled with train imagery.

I briefly considered attending the funeral (hoping to catch a glimpse of the widow in her weeds), but the newspapers announced that the ceremony was to be a private one. I contented myself therefore with writing a simple note offering my condolences.

Weeks and then months passed; Joan Tushy seemed to have vanished from my life. Then, one rainy Sunday night in April she appeared literally on my doorstep. The housemaster was out for the evening and I was on duty, assisted by one of the house prefects, a reliable but otherwise unprepossessing boy named Arthur Clegg. Shortly after ten o'clock, I was in the lavatory checking for cigarette smokers when Clegg entered in a state of excitement. "There's a lady at your door, sir," he said. "She's not wearing any shoes. I mean, she's holding her shoes in her hand." This remarkable intelligence unnerved me, though I affected an air of sangfroid in front of the flustered boy. I had no idea who my caller might be. No shoes? I thought at once of a mother deranged by her son's failure in English and now at my doorstep with scissors in her handbag. But that notion was absurd; I hadn't failed anyone in years. Then, too, the very appearance of a female at The Gannymede was something of an occasion, since aside from Bea Corcoran and the two ancient nurses in the infirmary, we seldom saw women during term time.

I hurried down the hallway followed by the Clegg boy. Joan Tushy was standing by my doorstep in her stocking feet. She was wearing a trench coat and had just taken off a kerchief. Her hair was bleached and she was brown as a nut. Smiling crookedly she held up her shoes. She looked a bit tight.

"Hello, Philip," she said. "Just passing through. Wondered if you could warm up a lonely wayfarer with a drink. I stepped in a goddamn puddle when I got out of the car."

Arthur Clegg seemed transfixed by her presence.

"Nothing," I said, "would give me greater pleasure." Turning to Clegg, I told him to check the rooms and go to bed.

In my apartment Joan placed her shoes by the radiator. "Let me take your coat," I said.

"Ah no," she said. "Not for the nonce, Philip, if you don't mind. I'll just walk around a bit in it. Been sitting all day and my bottom's numb."

"As you wish," I said. "A little whiskey?"

"Lovely." She was walking about and looking at my pictures. In the kitchen I made drinks and listened to her tell me that she was on the way home from Mexico. She appeared in the doorway and smiled. "I stayed last night in this ghastly hotel near Lexington, Kentucky. A man tried to pick me up in the restaurant."

"Is that so?"

"Yes, that is so, dear Philip," she said, taking a glass of whiskey. "Then it rained all bloody afternoon on the New York Thruway. It got me down a bit. I didn't really feel up to my place right off, if you know what I mean. I trust I'm not imposing."

"Not at all," I said. "I'm delighted to see you." I hesitated and then said, "I was, of course, sorry to hear about your husband. It must have been an awful ordeal for you."

"Yes, it was," she said. "It was all really too ghastly for

words." She leaned against the doorjamb and stared at her drink. She didn't look in the least remorseful. "I mean," she continued, "the poor sod needn't have gone about it that way. I mean, there are ever so many more pleasant ways to go about it." She tapped the glass against a long tooth. "You know, I've often wondered about those people whose job it is to pick up the pieces."

"Yes," I said. "It must be dreadful. I suppose one gets used to it."

"I suppose one does," Joan said, "but fancy picking up bits of a person who's just been belted by a train doing sixty miles an hour. I've thought about it a lot recently. Dreamt about it, even. Probably will for the rest of my life, I shouldn't wonder."

"Would you like another?" I asked.

"Oh, yes, please," she said, handing me her glass.

"You're sure I can't take your coat?" I asked.

"In a moment, my dear fellow," she said, looking around my kitchen. "You certainly keep a neat ship, Philip. The dishes all done. Everything tidy." I don't know why people like myself are always put on the defensive for being orderly, but it seems we are.

"I seldom use the kitchen," I said. "I take most of my meals in the dining hall. And then Mrs. Spinnaker comes in to clean for me every day. It goes with living in residence."

"Ah, I see," said Joan, opening a cupboard door. "But even if you didn't have Mrs. Spinnaker, I should think you'd run a very neat and tidy little ship."

"Perhaps I would," I said sharply, handing her a fresh drink.

She laid a hand on my arm. "Most men in my life have

been slovenly. Artistic types. My first husband was a sculptor. An Englishman. Filthy sod. Never washed his feet."

"Shall we go into the living room?" I said. "I'm sure we'd be much more comfortable. And you can just as easily admire my tidiness from there."

Joan laughed and linked her arm in mine. "Now, don't be bitchy, Philip. You sound like an old queen, you know. And I'm sure you don't want to sound like that."

I said nothing. The woman both irritated and enchanted me.

"Of course," she said, "Dwight and I were not really hitting it off these past couple of years. I took several lovers. I told you about Dwight's little problem at your party, did I not?"

"Yes."

"It was all in his head, of course. That's what the psychiatrist told him. Absolutely nothing wrong with his thing. In the first years of our marriage he was top-hole. But then he lost interest. The only thing that got him going was adolescents. We holidayed once in Greece. There was a little street urchin. Perhaps fourteen, maybe not even that. The three of us went back to the hotel." She laughed. "My dear Philip, I'm sorry. I've shocked you."

"Not at all," I lied. Joan sipped her drink.

"My first husband Jerome was a pig. Physically and emotionally a pig. Oh, these artists, Philip, they are so self-centred. We lived in this squalid little bed-sitter in Shepherd's Bush. That's in London."

"Well, I know that, for heaven's sake. I may seem to you to have lived a sheltered life. But I have been places.

As a matter of fact, I've been to England a number of times. Also Bermuda, the West Indies." I didn't bother mentioning that these trips had been with Captain Hale and the cricket team.

Joan looked thoughtful; I wasn't sure she'd even heard me. "While I was sitting in that rotten little room, Jerome was fucking art students at a friend's studio. And me a poor innocent girl from Sydney, only a few months in England. Then Dwight came along. He and others were giving a reading at some hall. Sponsored by Friends of the Commonwealth or some such nonsense. I read about it on the back page of the *New Statesman*, which Jerome regularly filched from the neighbourhood library. There it was amidst the notices for meetings of the Friends of Trotsky or the Armenian Relief League. I thought I'd go along. There might be a few fellow Australians there. What a funny evening it was, Philip! Shopgirls and library clerks and pale young men in pullovers applauding like mad while a big black fellow in a colourful dashiki read out this rubbish about freedom and slicing off the white man's balls to get it. Then there was a funny little man from New Zealand who wrote poems about garden vegetables. And Dwight in his lumber jacket and his poems about the wheat fields and the sound of the freight train whistle under the big sky. He quite overwhelmed me. That voice. He wore hair in those days, of course, the shaven-head business was a recent development. After the reading I introduced myself to him over coffee. Within the hour we were in his hotel room fucking like the prairie wind he was always going on about. Of course, his poetry had no bite in those days. No *snap*. After he met me he did his best work. It was I who released the erotic energy in him. During those first years the poetry poured out of him. Within a year he had completed *Mrs. Donovan's Tiny Bird.* He dedicated that volume to me and rightly so. Then *Beast Music*, of course. That made him famous and I fear ruined him. Dwight was never the same chap after *Beast Music.*"

"Well," I said, "it certainly brought him fame. In this country, at least. And," I added gallantly, "if you inspired him, and I have no reason to doubt your word, then you are to be congratulated."

Joan was still musing, staring at the floor. "Yes," she said. "I suppose I am. My poor, poor Dwight." Looking up, she suddenly finished her drink and brightened. "Well, what's past is prologue. Someday I shall write my autobiography, revealing all the sordid details of my curious and interesting life. But not until I'm at least three score and ten. An old lady with liver spots and great jangling bracelets on my wrists. Young people will visit me in the afternoons to hear me speak of my adventures. And in my apartment, surrounded by large plants and cages of brilliantly coloured birds, I shall entertain them in a voice hoarse from a lifetime of cigarettes and gin. Behind me and probably dead, my various lovers and husbands, several dozen at least." She laughed loudly. "The best is yet to come, dear Philip. During these past few weeks in Mexico I have cast off mourning. I am now ready to resume whatever is worth resuming."

"Hurrah," said I, raising my glass.

"Yes," said Joan. She arose unsteadily. "Hurrah, indeed. Hurrah for merriment in all its various guises including the pleasures of the flesh." With that pronouncement she shucked off the trench coat to reveal only a scarlet merry-widow corset with black straps and lacings. "My dear Philip," she announced, "I put it to you that we are going to have some rather naughty fun."

"You may certainly count me in," I replied. I crossed the room at once and we embraced with ardour. I make no apologies for the use of that fine old-fashioned word.

"My darling," said Joan. "I've wanted you desperately since the night of your soiree. You were so beautiful standing by the leaded window in your blazer and grey flannels. Do you mind terribly my saying that? About your being beautiful, I mean?"

"Not in the least," I said.

"You looked so *restful*. And I'm so weary of touchy, flamboyant men. They've all been so *unstaid*. My life needs tidying and constancy, dearest Philip. Where is *la chambre à coucher*?"

As we undressed in the bedroom Joan excited me dreadfully by whispering lewd words into my ear. In a trice we were making intricate and wonderful love. Then, in the midst of this rapture, levered into a position beyond my powers to describe, and approaching a plane of carnal bliss that must never again be hoped for in fear of disappointment, I heard the doorbell. Very nearly maddened by lust and rage, I clutched my bathrobe and, bent over, scuttled to the front door, looking, I imagine, not unlike some freak of nature, a giant, obscene land crab. I left Joan convulsed with mirth. "Who the devil is that?" I shouted through the door.

"It's Arthur Clegg, sir," said Arthur Clegg. "I've checked the rooms, sir. May I go to bed now?" This was a meaningless query inasmuch as he did so every night of his life.

"Yes," I yelled. "Go to bed, Clegg. Go to bed at once or I shall open this door and hit you with one of my walking sticks. I'll maim you, Clegg."

"Yes, sir," replied Clegg. "Thank you, sir. Good night, sir."

Groaning, I hastened to the bedroom where I found Joan sitting up smoking a cigarette. She was tapping the ashes into one of my pots of African violets on the windowsill. "You musn't do that," I cried. "Those are very sensitive plants. They're easily upset by foreign matter in the soil. I'll get you an ashtray."

"Oh, my dearest," said Joan. "I'm so sorry. I had no idea. How thoughtless of me! I'll put this nasty old thing out." She took several large puffs. "There's so much I have to learn. Will you teach me, my precious?"

"Perhaps," I said, handing her an ashtray.

She extinguished the cigarette and waved away the smoke. Smiling at me she said, "But time enough for that. Let us now resume the festivities. Did the Venetian Concertina charm you, my darling?"

Six

It goes without saying that it did, and over the next two years I would be charmed by a score of variations. The difficulty lay in the fact that so would many others. Even as I walked along the beach on that first evening in Cozumel, I imagined my wife and the Americans coupling in some ingenious arrangement under the moonlight. The cuckold always suspects the worst.

After dinner I had taken aspirin for my headache and gone for a brief walk. In the luminous tropical evening other visitors strolled by the sea. Like myself they were doubtless enchanted by the novelty of walking along a beach on a night in February. In front of the hotel was a small jetty where the glass bottom boats moored. The hotel lights played along this wooden ramp and over the water. Standing there I watched the rockfish darting about as they fed in the green-lighted water. After a moment I was joined by a middle-aged man from Japan who sold robots. He informed me of this as we both gazed down at the fishes. Mr. Yoshimodo told me that he had done excellent business in Dallas and Houston and had decided to treat himself to a week's holiday before returning to Japan. He was an amiable man and invited me to have a drink with him in his room. I declined, however, for I was fairly certain that Mr. Yoshimodo was a homosexual. I have an instinct about such persons.

In my room I lay on the bed and browsed through a textbook of literary criticism for senior students. The book had been sent to me by a publisher in the hope that I would find it suitable for classroom use and purchase two hundred copies. I fell asleep over an essay on Mark Twain written by some man who teaches at Hullabaloo U.

At the best of times I am a light sleeper and so I was easily wakened by Joan's voice outside the door. Lying with my eyes closed I also recognized the voice of Ted Hacker. I heard Joan say, "Well, Dwight would have been all for it, but I'm not so sure about dear old Philip."

Dear old Philip! At once I opened my eyes. Something was afoot! From the bed I watched through narrowed eyes as they entered the room. Joan had thrown a sweater across her shoulders. An hibiscus bloomed in her hair. Hacker had abandoned the Bermuda shorts and now wore a pair of large baggy trousers secured by an elastic waistband. On his head was an enormous dark sombrero fringed with silver tassels.

"Hullo, hullo," said Joan. "What have we here? Having a bit of a snooze, dear heart? It's only eleven o'clock, you know."

"Yes," I said. "Dear old Philip was having a bit of a snooze. And, having just looked at his watch, is well aware that it's only eleven o'clock. Whatever that has to do with anything."

Joan stood over me smiling. "I was only thinking that you mightn't sleep well later on, my darling. You know how you suffer with insomnia."

"Why not," I said, "mention my various other neurotic

symptoms to our guest? I'm sure Mr. Hacker is interested in the fact that I don't sleep well, and that from time to time I must take powders for my stomach. Also that by times I have a cranky bowel."

Hacker was grinning, his face partly in shadows under the ridiculous hat.

"What do you say, Phil?" Extending his arms he began to dance sideways across the room singing "South of the Border, Down Mexico Way." For a large man he was graceful and light in motion. Joan watched him admiringly.

"Where is your wife?" I asked.

"Getting into her bathing suit," said Hacker. He was now dancing away from us. "We're all going for a swim."

"It's Ted's idea," said Joan, "and I think it's simply marvellous. Have you seen the full moon, Philip? It's perfect for a midnight swim."

"A little dip under the tropical stars," said Hacker, who had stopped singing and dancing. Like a child balancing on a railway track, he was now slowly walking across the room. Arms still extended he stared at the floor following some imaginary line, the peculiar fellow.

Joan was enormously excited by this business of swimming in the dark. "Ted says there's a wonderful beach just a hundred yards down the road. He walked there this afternoon."

"Are you quite certain this is a sound idea?" I asked. "It seems to me . . ." I hesitated. I am cautious, but not craven, though people often persist in confusing prudence with timidity. "I mean, isn't it a bit foolhardy? I'm thinking of how one is often warned about venturing into strange waters after dark."

Hacker stopped his balancing act and lowered the brim of his sombrero so that I could not discern his face. Joan had plucked the hibiscus from her hair and was now smelling the flower.

"Don't sharks feed at night near shore?" I asked. "In that film *Jaws*, a girl went swimming . . ."

Hacker laughed. "There are no sharks in these parts, Phil."

"Perhaps, but I'm still not convinced it's wise. But why don't the three of you go ahead?"

"More fun with four," said Hacker. "Don't be a party-poop, Phil."

"Well," announced Joan. "You can do as you please, darling. But I'm going to get into my bathing costume."

"Goody, goody gumdrops," said Hacker, pushing the big hat back on his head. He watched Joan walk to the bathroom, then came over and sat on the edge of my bed. Placing a hand on my thigh he said, "Now, Phil, the gals are looking forward to this event. That's all they talked about on the ride back from town. You don't want to disappoint them, do you?" He was now squeezing my thigh. He winked. "And you never know what might develop. I don't how your wife feels about certain things, but I can assure that the Cork is a fun person."

"Just what in hell are you suggesting, Hacker?" I asked.

"Please call me Ted, Phil." My leg was growing numb.

"Please take your bloody hand off my leg," I said.

Hacker squeezed harder and spoke in the voice of a tiny child. "Not unwess you pway wiv us."

"For heaven's sake, Hacker, you're hurting me."

"You promised to call me Ted."

"All right, *Ted*. Now please stop it."

"Hi, everybody," came a small voice from the doorway. It was Corky Hacker. Her husband's hand sprang from my thigh and, as though it were afire, he began to shake it and blow on the fingertips. He winked at me again. "We're gonna have ourselves a time, Phil." He turned toward his wife, who wore jeans and a sweatshirt. With the headband around her frizzed hair she looked like a teenager. "Hi, honey," said Hacker. "Would you believe the bad news? Phil doesn't want to go swimming with us."

"Ah gee, Philip," said Corky Hacker. She had chewing gum in her mouth. "It'll be fun." I must confess that I found her oddly alluring. In fact, she reminded me of the girl with whom I had my first sexual encounter donkey's years ago. Oh, allow a murderer to reveal a sexual episode from his past. Why, it even may cast (psychiatrists may remove their jackets and make notes if they wish) some scattered light on the penumbra of my fiendishness!

When I was thirteen, I, along with a busload of Gannymedians, journeyed down the road to St. Melody's for a school dance. Dances between the two schools were held three or four times a year; indeed, mergers between families often had their genesis in these innocent outings. It was my first dance and I remember how clumsy I felt in the presence of those composed young females in their cashmere sweaters and pleated tartan skirts. I dutifully pushed several of them around the gymnasium under the watchful eye of the chaperones.

At intermission I walked out and into a May evening

that was richly fragrant with lilacs. I was then experimenting with tobacco and so I strolled in the direction of the school gates, thinking it might be safer to smoke beyond the grounds. Bolder boys had already taken refuge behind various bits of shrubbery, and you could see their cigarettes glowing like fireflies in the dark. By the gates I noticed a slight figure standing in the shadows near one of the large cement urns that flanked the entrance. As I drew nearer, I saw that she was about my age, an unkempt urchin in a shapeless dress, and barelegged. On her feet were a pair of black, low-cut shoes (popular among teenaged girls at the time and called, I believe, ballerinas). The urchin was chewing gum.

With her arms crossed over her chest she watched my approach. From the light of a street lamp I could see a look of immense disdain on her face. I expect she was waiting for me to tell her to get off the property, though I had no right to do so. Feeling magnanimous and adult, I offered her a cigarette, which she took without a word. Leaning against the gate railings we smoked in silence—this aloof waif and I—strangers and worlds apart, yet united somehow by a mysterious and burgeoning intimacy. In a matter of minutes we were thrusting our tongues down one another's throats. She gave off the strange odour of damp boards and sweat. She whispered that she wouldn't fuck me unless I had a safe. The obscenity made me slightly delirious; in those days you barely heard the word uttered by a boy (certainly not a Gannymedian), let alone a girl. She told me I could touch her but only if I didn't rub too hard. Good heavens above, reader, think of me in the circumstances—a chaste private-school lad who knew not this nor that of matters carnal!

Seated on the damp grass I inserted my hand into her bloomers and massaged her barely hirsute genital while, with gum snapping, she whispered filthy words into my burning ear. After what seemed like hours of ecstasy (the dance had resumed and the band seemed to play forever a tune called "Cruising Down the River"), my lover sighed out a tiny orgasm while I enjoyed the most monstrous ejaculation of my brief life. We clung to one another until we heard "God Save the King" (yes, George VI was on the throne) and parted wordlessly, she walking through the gates to who knows where and I heading for the bus parked near the gymnasium, straightening my blazer and flannels, but walking at a peculiar angle, the wilted head of my little dummy pasted to my Jockey shorts.

And in the El Gringo Hotel, Corky Hacker put me so in mind of that long-ago evening in May! Why, she could have been the waif's daughter! In short, I consented to go with them but warned that I would not venture into the sea.

"Fair enough," boomed Hacker, withdrawing from his voluminous pants a pint bottle of whiskey. "Who's for a drink?"

"I shall most certainly take advantage of your kindness," said Joan, coming from the bathroom in a rose-coloured bikini that I'm certain would not have been allowed in areas reserved for family bathing.

Hacker produced the expected wolf whistle. "Ladies

and gentlemen, will you look at her!" He began to play an imaginary trombone, stopping only to sing, "Here she comes! Miss Americaaaa!" Corky Hacker applauded. "Let's get the show on the road, keeds," said her husband, watching carefully as my wife climbed into slacks and sweater.

Seven

"Watch out for these taxis," Hacker yelled, as we walked along the edge of the highway in a single file. "These little people seem to go haywire when they get behind the wheel of a car." This was true. The island apparently had no speed limit, and now and then taxis carrying passengers to and from the hotels along the beach rushed past us. As we stepped into the roadside grass to avoid these vehicles, it occurred to me that along such a thoroughfare an accident could easily befall the unwary. In the dark of night a person might stumble (be nudged?) into the path of an onrushing Pontiac.

Such a mishap would be attended by terrible confusion. There would be the inevitable screeching of brakes followed by the driver running back, pulling his hair, and calling on Our Lady of Guadalupe to intercede on his behalf. "Mother of God, señor, it was *el accidente*. I am sorry but I did not see her until the last minute. She walked into the headlights. And for this I will lose my licence and my living. It is forbidden to kill a tourist. I have nine children at home, señor." All this to the distraught man bent over the body of his wife. Alas, he could find no pulse. And now they were joined by the passengers, decent Americans all. "You poor, poor man." That from an attractive blonde hausfrau in her middle years. Her husband, a beefy good-natured man, would tell me to "take it easy, fellah." Later they would guide me to a grassy knoll where I would be allowed to go to pieces by myself.

Such an event, however, could not come to pass on such a lucent evening. Under the full moon the road lay stark and white through the jungle. In front of me, Hacker's sombrero sat upon his head like a great dark wheel. We had wordlessly divided into two pairs, and Hacker and Joan had lengthened the distance between themselves and Corky Hacker and me. We walked, listening to the cries of night birds and to rustlings in the jungle. Where there were no cars to be seen, I moved alongside Corky Hacker, and after a while she slipped her arm through mine. Hacker already had his arm around my wife's shoulders. They were laughing a great deal. And I, why, I was overcome by a sense of wonder that left me exhilarated. Normally at eleven-thirty on a Sunday night in February you will find me reading in bed with a plate of arrowroot biscuits and a cup of cocoa by my elbow. Joan always watches some tripe about Lady Cynthia or Sir Charles on *Masterpiece Theatre*, and then sits at her vanity applying various cleansing unguents to her face and throat. Intercourse might very well follow and the exertions required often leave me dazed and anxious for my heart.

How different from that scene of dreary Canadian domesticity was walking through a tropical night with a beautiful young woman! From time to time we looked at one another and smiled. Finally she said, "Isn't it a wonderful night, Philip?"

"It most assuredly is," I said. "Dramatically beautiful."

She sighed. "We sure don't get anything like this in

Lincoln." With that she tightened her grip on my arm and, leaning her head against my shoulder, looked up at the moon. "I can see the old man in the moon."

"Yes, indeed," I said. "The old rascal has his eye on us."

"Do you know something?" she asked.

"What?"

"When I first saw you in the hotel dining room I said to Ted, 'I'll bet that man over there in the blue blazer is a professor or something.' You looked so distinguished."

"Thank you."

"You must read a lot of books, Philip."

"Well, I have done, I suppose," I said. "Mostly in literature. I'm very narrowly educated, I'm afraid. Know almost nothing about science, for example."

"I certainly admire educated people," said Corky Hacker. "I'm taking some courses at the university. I don't want to always be a dope."

"And why do you consider yourself a dope?"

"Oh, I don't know, I just do. Everybody always seems to know more than I do about things." She laughed. "Except, of course, for one thing."

"Oh," said I. "And what might that be?"

"Oh, I'll never tell." She laughed. I found myself stirred by her presence. I am sure that this was due in part to our being tourists in the tropics. I once read an article which stated that a rich sense of abandonment often accompanies a visitor to warm lands and this, in turn, stimulates the gonads.

We were now following the others through a narrow path to the sea which lay gleaming beyond, under the enormous moon. Around the bend of the shore were the lights from our hotel. As I followed Corky Hacker along the path I asked her what sort of books she liked reading. She stopped and I bumped into her. Looking back at me she smiled and whispered, "I love books about screwing. Really dirty stories. Isn't that awful!" She laughed and I felt her breath on my face. Then she turned, saying, "We'd better catch up. Teddy and Joan will be in the water by now."

But as it developed, they were not, though both had shed most of their clothes and stood like savages on the pale sand. Hacker wore a pair of bikini net swimming trunks that emphasized the heavy bulge of his prominent beasthood.

"My, my," said Joan. "You're a big one, aren't you?"

Hacker grinned. "Hubba hubba hubba ding dong bell! That's what my mom used to say to me on Friday nights when I'd be going out to the high-school dance or the malt shop. I understand that as an expression of admiration it had considerable vogue during the late forties."

He began to walk into the water. In the windless night the surf broke gently against his legs. "I'll bet," said Hacker, "they're freezing their knackers back home about now." He dove at once into the dark sea and for several moments was underwater before surfacing a good distance from shore. He waved to us. "Get in here, y'all. It's great."

Corky Hacker cupped her hands to her mouth. "You just be careful now, Ted Hacker," she scolded. Her husband swam toward shore and began to splash Joan, who was stepping into the water.

"Ted, no," she cried delightedly. They might have been man and wife.

"Get in here, Joanie," yelled Hacker. "And where's my Cork? I want my Cork."

"I'm coming, Teddy bear," said his wife, who now stood beside me unbuttoning her jeans. I'd been rather looking forward to this, but in fact as she stepped from her clothes Corky Hacker revealed nothing more startling than a one-piece white swimsuit. In this modest costume from the fifties (I thought of the old aquatic star of films—Esther Williams) she joined the others, squealing with joy as they flung water in her direction.

Sitting on the beach and watching the three of them splash about in the sea, I experience a sense of benevolent ease. Why, after all, shouldn't people play in the water in the dead of night? Such activity was clearly discouraged in any manual on water safety I'd read, but was it not perhaps a good idea to break the rules now and again? There was much about my settled state that might reward periodic scrutiny. A lifetime spent in an institution promotes habits of order and discipline, and without a doubt these are admirable qualities. But could it not also leave the spirit undernourished and wanting in playfulness? I ended this colloquy with myself by quietly agreeing that it was possible.

As they swam about, Joan called to me. "Oh, do come in, Philip, the water is marvellous."

"Thanks, no," I replied. "In any event, I have no bathing trunks."

"Well, wear your shorts, for goodness sakes." For some reason this suggestion provoked a great deal of laughter amongst all three.

"Another time perhaps," I called. "Enjoy yourselves." After all, I thought, all three were younger than I and it was surely more fitting that they should cavort in the sea. Nor, when it came to that, were they probably such bad folk. I concluded that murdering Joan was perhaps extreme. That she was vulgar and loud and would possibly occasion my ruin at The Gannymede was undeniable. And regarding that subject I was again moved to wonder whether she had had intercourse with the Hotchkiss boy. In my agreeable humour I was inclined to doubt it. Not even Joan would go so far as to involve herself with a student. Yet the expression on the boy's face on my doorstep that night had suggested triumph and unbelievable luck. As for Hacker, he was unquestionably a boor, though amiable enough. That business of squeezing my leg in the hotel room was probably caused by too much drink. And his wife was a sweet creature; someone to enjoy a little flirtation with over the week. I resolved to get on better with them.

"I do wish you'd come in, Philip," called Joan. "You're missing out on the treat of a lifetime."

"No, thank you. I'm quite content right here. I'm enjoying the wonderful night."

"Oh, do be a sport, Philip," she cried.

"Another time perhaps."

"We all think you should come in, Philip," said Hacker. He sounded mildly resentful.

"Please, Philip," said Joan. "It's ever so nice."

"More fun with four," said Corky Hacker.

"I'm sure," I said, "that you can all get along very nicely without me."

"Maybe we can and then maybe we can't," Hacker

said mysteriously. I didn't much care for the tone of his voice.

The three of them had now stopped swimming and were talking among themselves. Their laughter travelled over the dark water. A moment later all three arose and walked toward me without a word. As they stood over me their silence seemed weighted with menace, and I looked up uneasily at their glistening bodies. Hacker's costume was now nothing more than an obscene wet codpiece.

"Had enough, then?" I asked.

"Now, Phil," said Hacker. "We don't think you're being very cooperative. You are, after all, on vacation. It follows naturally that you should join in the fun and not sit here on the sand like some old poop of a bystander. What do you say?"

"What's this all about, then?" I asked. I was annoyed by his presumption about what I should or should not do on my holidays. All three continued to stare down at me.

"Now, Phil," said Hacker, smiling. "We think you should get out of these duds and come for a swim."

"What?" I laughed. "Don't be ridiculous, Hacker. I've already told you I've no wish to go bathing tonight."

Hacker wagged a finger at me. "Now remember. You promised to call me Ted back at the hotel. He really did, girls. Ooo is not being vewy fewindly, Phil."

Corky Hacker expelled a short bark of laughter and covered her mouth. How I regretted my earlier fascination with this shallow little creature!

"What seems to be happening," I said, "is that matters are getting out of hand. I suggest that everyone's had a little too much to drink. I'm going back to the hotel."

"Now, ladies," said Hacker, "it's one for the money

and it's two for the show. It's three to get ready and away we go." And with the end of the nonsensical rhyme he leapt astride my chest, his huge bag of sodden parts mere inches from my face. He had seized my wrists in his powerful hands while the women pinned my legs.

"For the love of God," I gasped. "Have you all taken leave of your senses?"

"Bind fast his corky arms," cried Hacker. "That's from Shakespeare, pal."

"Get off me, damn it!" I demanded.

"Cease and desist," said Hacker. "Let's keep the peace here. None but the brave deserves the fair. Do you know where that famous quotation comes from, Phil? I understand you teach English in a boys' school. Me, I sell pills for a living."

"Let me up, goddamn it!"

"The quotation is from *Alexander's Feast*. By that estimable Restoration poet John Dryden, who alas is seldom read nowadays. But then we live in a base age. Now stop your struggling, Phil, or I'll crush your carpuses. Or carpi in the plural, I suppose. Wrists to the layman. I was once a medical student. Also a guard with a great Nebraska team. Go, you Cornhuskers, go go go!"

"This is battery, pure and simple," I shouted. "You are risking a charge."

Hacker looked behind him. "All right, ladies, to your appointed tasks. Remove the patient's shoes, socks, and trousers."

"Are you all mad?" I cried. "Joan, I insist that you stop this foolishness."

"Oh, for once in your life be a sport, Philip," said Joan, laughing.

"Yes," said Hacker, grinning down at me. "Don't be a filly dud dud. I mean a fuddy-dud, Phil." His grip burned my wrists.

"This is insupportable," I yelled.

Hacker began to sing "Embraceable You" while the two women removed everything below my waist save my candy-striped boxer shorts. It crossed my mind that by sheer bad luck I had stumbled across a pair of psychotics. It was criminal how the authorities nowadays allowed deranged persons to walk abroad assaulting innocent citizens. But how then to account for Joan's participation in their villainies? No matter, for I knew I would never forgive her for this. If I didn't murder her, I would divorce her. A more sensible course. Upon my return to Canada I would get in touch with Ross Parry. It would cause a minor scandal at the school. Any number of "I told you so's" would be uttered in the Common Room. But there was bound to be a certain amount of sympathy too.

After I was nearly naked, Hacker said, "Now don't do anything foolish, Phil, while I remove the rest of your garments." By now, however, I had decided to rise above their childish behaviour. I would endure the ordeal with as much dignity as could be mustered under the ridiculous circumstances. And so I said nothing while Hacker peeled off my shirt. Joan watched with a foxy grin, while Corky Hacker gazed down at her foot as it described a circle in the sand. She, at least, now seemed slightly embarrassed by the incident. After Hacker had removed my clothes, I said, "Are you quite finished now?"

"Quite quite," said Hacker.

"Fine," I said. "Now, to satisfy your foolish whims, I'll go into the water."

Hacker was at once eager and friendly. "Listen, Phil, it's great, you'll love it, believe me."

They watched as I strode to the water. I would not give them the satisfaction of seeing me appear in the least hesitant and so I plunged into the sea, surfacing to applause. Having participated, I believed that I would now be allowed to return to my clothes. However, this was not to be. As I made for shore something gripped my ankles and pulled me backward and beneath the surface. Terrified, I held my breath as I was towed underwater. The hands then released me and deftly stripped off my underpants. Clawing my way to the surface I trod water, sputtering and naked. A moment later Hacker's head appeared a few feet away. The blond hair was plastered to his skull. "Hi, pal!" he said.

"You bastard, give me back my shorts."

"You have to say the magic word."

I began to swim for shore. Although I am strong in the water (Gannymede Second Team, 1953) I was no match for Hacker, who fell in beside me using the backstroke. His long pale arms thrashed the water like paddlewheels. Looking over at me he said, "You don't like me, do you, Phil?"

"How could anyone like a person who has just tried to drown him?" I asked.

Hacker laughed. "I didn't try to drown you, Phil. I was only kidding. Why would I try to drown you, for crying out loud? That's crazy."

"I don't know why you're behaving like this," I said, trying to keep the self-pity out of my voice.

"I'm not such a bad guy," said Hacker. "I've read Proust. I didn't like him, but I've read him."

Ignoring this, I concentrated on swimming. I was astonished at how far he had dragged me from the shore, for I could see the two women waving at us. As we drew closer, Hacker said, "What do you say we moon the girls?" Again I said nothing. "Watch this," said Hacker, rolling over and sinking from sight. A moment later a pair of large white buttocks emerged. Joan and Corky Hacker laughed and clapped their hands. Hacker's backside disappeared and then he surfaced directly in my path. "Your turn, Phil," he said. I stopped to tread water. I was winded by this sudden and violent exercise.

"Look," I said, "I don't know what your game is, but I'm sick of it. You could have drowned me back there. And now you've taken my underpants! What's all this supposed to prove? I don't understand this kind of bullying at all."

"Hey, come on now, big guy," said Hacker. "I was just kidding." He held up my boxer shorts and absurdly wrung the water from them before returning them to me. As I struggled into them (not as easy while treading water as you might imagine), Hacker said, "No hard feelings, I hope. Can we shake on that, Phil?"

"I'm not shaking your hand," I said. "It would be sheer hypocrisy."

"But it's a symbol of friendship," said Hacker. "Tried and true. Down through the ages this simple gesture has said, Accept me, for I have no weapons and I intend no malice."

"No," I said firmly. "Now will you get out of my way? I've had enough of your nonsense."

"Please, Phil. A simple clasping of our hands signifying accord and goodwill."

“I will not shake your hand, Hacker.”

He uttered a terrible cry, a primeval wail of pain and rage, and I was again underwater. After several seconds Hacker pulled me to the surface, but only long enough for me to take a few breaths and then I was under again. He then released me, and I arose spluttering and furious while the women cheered. I suppose they thought we were playing some game. Ted Hacker grinned and extended his hand. “Are we pals or not?”

With considerable reluctance I shook the large hand, expecting yet another of his idiotic tricks. But his grip was surprisingly gentle. “You’re okay, Philippo,” he said. “Let’s go and have us a drink.”

Eight

Mr. Humberto was only partly right in his forecast of my immediate future. Two weeks ago an inspector of detectives and his assistant completed their investigation of the crime. They were sinister-looking men in their shiny suits and sunglasses and they questioned me for hours, but they did *not* beat me. After they finished their interrogation, the assistant attached a handcuff to his wrist and mine, and the three of us were flown in a small plane south to the state capital where I now await my trial.

Life at the prison here at Chetumal is not so bad, especially since the arrival of a large money order from my aunts. With money you can live fairly comfortably in a Mexican jail. It provides you with those little extras that make life bearable. I now have, for example, a servant. Miguel is a very old man with a walleye. He hangs about the place in the hope of running errands for prisoners with money. The guards tolerate his presence, though I imagine Miguel pays them a portion of his earnings. Mexican officialdom seems quite comfortable with this kind of arrangement.

Miguel has been invaluable, bringing me fresh washed fruit to supplement a diet weighted heavily in favour of beans and tortillas. Actually the food is not markedly inferior to the fare served at The Gannymede. My bowels have adjusted to the climate and the water, and I am in good health. My spirits have improved, too, thanks largely to Miguel, who is a cheerful soul and regards me with considerable awe. He has told me that over the years most of the gringos he has served have been young Americans facing drug charges. "Dirty young men, Señor Bannister," said Miguel, turning his bad eye from me. "They give you a few centavos if you fetch them Coca-Cola or chewing gum. And what are they here for?" He spat on the stone floor. "Drugs! That is why it is such an honour to serve a gentleman like you, Señor Bannister. Someone who has committed a real crime."

I was touched by the old man's words, but what has really heartened me over the past few days has been the arrival of a dozen books. I had asked Miguel if he could find me something to read, expecting him to turn up with a few old copies of *Time* or *Newsweek*. Instead he appeared with a veritable treasure trove: what was left of the contents of an Edwardian library once owned by a long dead Englishwoman, a Miss Dodge who, for reasons never made clear to me, resided in these parts for years. Miguel once worked as her gardener. He did not say how he came by Miss Dodge's books, though in all likelihood he stole them. He told me that most of them had been ruined by mildew and certainly the ones he brought me are in sorry shape. Yet what a source of joy they are for a middle-aged schoolmaster far from home!

I am rationing them and so each day I open a few mouldy pages, though sometimes I forget myself and devour whole chapters of Bulwer-Lytton's *The Last Days of Pompeii* or Trollope's *Framley Parsonage* or *The Cloister and the Hearth*. Among others is the 1909 edition of Palgrave's *Golden Treasury* and Edgar Rice

Burroughs's *Tarzan of the Apes*, first published in the year that Great Britain went to war against the Central Powers. It is fortunate for me that Miss Dodge chose to live in this region and hire Miguel for her gardener!

Along with the money order came a letter from Aunty Fay. She is a year younger than her sister and still writes in a clear, firm hand despite her four score years. Aunty Fay was sorry that they could not visit me, but was sure I would understand how difficult driving was in the winter. I suspect that a little dust has gathered in the corridors of her memory, for neither of them has operated an automobile in years and the family Packard was sold at auction in 1969. Aunty Fay mentioned that they were keeping busy in the Land of Smiles. Aunty Flo had given a concert in the Sun Parlour and this had been politely received, though it was hinted that the music of Bach and Scarlatti was perhaps imperfectly understood and less appreciated than the hymns offered by one Vera Hoople, who appears to be an enemy. My aunts have also invented a new game (something to do with choosing colours) and Aunty Fay expressed the wish that I were there to play it with them. She ended her letter on the rather disturbing note of wondering what I thought they should do with their money in the unhappy event that I was executed or died in prison from a beating. Aunty Fay has a vivid imagination and in 1921 received an encouraging rejection letter from H. L. Mencken, who was then editing a magazine called *Smart Set*.

I sat for a long time holding the letter in my hand and thinking of my dear aunts at the Land of Smiles Retirement Facility. From their room you can look across the grounds to the benches under the trees. There in the fullness of summer, romance often flourishes amongst old folks who have retired from the fray. Now the benches would be filled with snow and the leafless trees would creak in the wind and the blue jays and chickadees would hop about on the feeder trays set out by the bird lovers. How I miss visiting my aunts for tea at the Land of Smiles. I always took along a dozen hermits or cream buns purchased at the Golden Oven. Sometimes I would take them a bottle of Harvey's Bristol Cream. During the first months of our marriage, Joan accompanied me, but somehow that never worked and, though my aunts were unfailingly polite and Joan was on her best behaviour, the atmosphere was often strained. I sensed that Joan felt I made too much of them, but, after all, as I pointed out to her many times, my aunts raised me.

My mother was unknown to me, having died in childbirth, and my fond and ineffectual father could no more look after a baby than a fish could wear a hat. When my aunts arrived from New York, he was hiding in a bedroom of the house on Sparrow Hill Road while downstairs a nurse fed me from a bottle. This was 1937. After spending much of that decade travelling in Europe, my aunts had settled in New York, where Aunty Flo was having the affair of a lifetime with a mad Russian émigré pianist. While she took lessons from the czarist, Aunty Fay wrote stories and worked in an advertising agency. At night there were parties in Greenwich Village where they met people like Delmore Schwartz and the prizefighter Primo Carnera. Aunty Fay once showed me a snapshot in which *both* she and Aunty Flo are being lifted into the air by the giant Italian. Yet they gave up this interesting bohemian life and without complaint returned to the family home to look after their brother and his son. They stayed until I was old enough to be enrolled as a boarder at The Gannymede, and afterward I spent my holidays and summers with them.

At the beginning of my eleventh year, my father's neurasthenia worsened and he was removed to a lunatic asylum, where he died of heart failure some ten years later. What seems to have hastened his collapse was the sale of the house next to us on Sparrow Hill Road, the old Fudge place. It was a stately brick mansion and it was bought by a man who had made a fortune selling automobiles. The fellow's wife immediately began to populate the spacious lawn and gardens with plaster objects that even our hedge could not conceal. There were swans and ducks and deer and several pickaninnies in jockey costumes. Each morning my poor father would stand in our library window which overlooked the salesman's garden. He would stand there in his old sweater coat with his hands clasped behind his back, watching the salesman's wife place another three-foot Venus de Milo near the sundial. And watching her he would grow increasingly melancholy. At night he took to slipping through the hedge and carrying off these objects; indeed, he was once apprehended in his dressing gown clutching Snow White and some of the Seven Dwarfs. He was let off with a warning. Finally one day, however, he was observed by early risers as he crouched near our verandah in the attitude of Rodin's *The Thinker*. He was naked as a babe. The salesman's wife screamed, and the police arrived and kindly took him away.

To see your naked father lifted into the cruiser by policemen (he would not suffer himself to be uncurled) was a searing experience for an eleven-year-old boy. Yet my aunts preferred to make light of the incident. Your father, they told me, has made a witty and pointed statement about bad taste and should be congratulated and not condemned. They also assured me that he would be far happier in an institution. As Aunty Fay said, "The mad, my dear Philip, often understand these things better than the rest of us."

To cheer me up, Aunty Flo played "Wedding at Troyhagen" and "Golliwogs on Parade," favourites of mine and compositions which even today I cannot listen to unmoved, seeing, as I hear them, the small child in the house on Sparrow Hill Road with his face pressed against the coloured glass of the hallway door. Is it any wonder that I love my aunts? And how painful it is to think I shall probably never see them again!

I visited them the day before we left on this wretched Mexican holiday. I was depressed beyond measure by Joan's indiscretions, and I feared her latest contretemps, once revealed, would ruin me at The Gannymede.

The truth is that Joan's infidelities were beginning to unsettle me. In the two years of our marriage I had endured quietly the gossip and the pitying glances. Joan had had affairs with an amateur theatre director named Don Whipple, someone in the local art gallery, our dentist, a young man who had published poetry in a magazine long since bankrupt, and probably many others whom I didn't know about. She had exhibited enough sense not to bother anyone on the faculty, though there was the usual flirting at staff parties. But aside from Milo Murdoch and his leer, there was no inspiration at The

Gannymede; boarding-school teachers are perhaps the world's most timid players in the game of dalliance.

I was prepared to live with Joan's philandering as long as the school was not involved. But then the damnable woman gave me cause for genuine anxiety. The night before I visited my aunts, a boy named Hotchkiss, captain of the hockey team, a handsome, dull eighteen-year-old, had come by my apartment seeking help with an essay. Apparently we had arranged this appointment some time ago, but it had completely slipped my mind. When Hotchkiss arrived, I was on my way out the door to a meeting of the Cricket Club (we were planning our annual tour to Bermuda). I apologized to Hotchkiss and told him to come back another night. Then, leaving him on my doorstep, I hurried away to Captain Hale's house, for I was already late and the old soldier does not like to be kept waiting.

The meeting, however, did not come to pass as the Captain's gout flared up and he was rendered *hors de combat*. A half hour later I returned to my apartment, where I encountered Ralph Hotchkiss putting on his jacket. My wife was nowhere to be seen. "What the devil are you doing here, Hotchkiss?" I asked. "I said another night, did I not?"

Hotchkiss flushed deeply. "Yes, sir. Sorry, sir." As he hurried past me, he wore a sleepy grin that was both insolent and sly. I pride myself on being observant and I believe I recognized in the youth's smile the seducer's pity for the cuckold. Ralph Hotchkiss, in every respect an unremarkable person, was experiencing a moment of rare victory; indeed, perhaps it would prove to be the most triumphant moment of his life. He had just had intercourse with a woman twice his age (I had no proof, of course) and he had cuckolded his English teacher. Such an event would be worth cherishing for the rest of his days. I saw Hotchkiss as an old bald man sitting in a leather chair in his club, chuckling over this evening of his youth. Leaning forward with a drop on the end of his nose to tell it all for the hundredth time. "By the lord, Harry, what a rogering I gave her that night! And right under the old master's nose!"

Standing by my window, I watched him run across the snow to Bung Hall. As he ran he jumped into the air and clicked his heels together. Hotchkiss, I predicted, would never again be as happy. But of more immediate concern to me was not Hotchkiss's eventual happiness, but whether he could keep his mouth shut. He was not a particularly sensitive boy, and it seemed reasonable to assume that in time he would want to share his *coup* with other members of the hockey team. In which case there would be a scandal. Sexual peccadilloes are *verboten* in a boarding school; the merest hint of an impropriety can whiten the hair of a headmaster overnight and crush a school's reputation. There is an excellent small school in western Canada that took years to recover from an imbroglio involving a master, the cook, several boys, and some pails of lard. I was therefore unnerved by this turn of events.

At first Joan denied everything. Yet coming from the bathroom she appeared a little disordered in aspect. Not expecting me home so soon, you see! After a moment I said, "Joan, if that boy should start talking, then you are looking at a ruined man. It will be all over the school within the hour and I shall never again be able to face my colleagues or the student body. I've told you time and time again about such eventualities and please don't look at me as though I'm being stuffy. You know perfectly well how ridicule has driven many a good man from pulpit or classroom. And let me remind you also that I am now in my middle years. I have spent the last twenty of them teaching at The Gannymede, but should the new headmaster, who appears not overly fond of me, ask for my resignation, I might have difficulty securing another position. Nor," I added nastily, "have I seen evidence that you are capable of supporting the household. So consider what might become of us, foolish lady. What could we do?"

It was always difficult to irritate Joan; she was invariably good-natured, I'll give her that. And by then she had composed herself. "We could do," she said, "what we should have done ages ago, and that's get out. Good heavens above, Philip, I'm forty years old and you're what? Forty-nine?"

"Six," I said. "I'm forty-six, Joan, as you very well know."

"Well, whatever," she said. "The question simply put, darling, is this. Do we want to spend the rest of our lives in this funny old place where *nothing* ever happens. I say nay. I say we should chuck the bloody lot and clear out. We could live in Veracruz. Or Toulouse. Or dear, dirty Dublin. Where I'll shake your shillelagh if you like." She laughed merrily.

"When I first met you, you told me that you wanted order and repose in your life. You said that, Joan."

"Yes, yes, yes, I know. But I miss the artistic endeavours in life too. I miss my painting. And you could write or something." She raised her arms to the ceiling. "I wish to paint again," she declared.

"Or look for other painters," I said. "Preferably male and under thirty." She stuck out her tongue at me. "And what, pray (angered, I can be a little grandiose, a rhetorical device well-polished over the years and meant to subdue classroom troublemakers), would we do for money in these exotic places?"

"Oh, come off it, Philip. Who is fooling whom? Or should that be who? No matter! Everyone knows that those dear old aunts of yours are loaded. When they're gone, you'll be a rich man. And they're devoted to you. Why not ask the old things for a little advance. Say, a hundred thousand? That should tide us over while we await grim news from the Land of Smiles."

"That," I said, "is a perfectly revolting idea."

"Nonsense. They'd be thrilled to bits if they thought you were going to take up as an author or something. A breath of fresh air for them."

"My aunts are devoted friends of the school. Four generations of Bannisters have attended The Gannymede and I am the only one who has taught here. My aunts are very proud of me. It would break their hearts if I were to leave, especially under questionable circumstances."

"My dear Philip," said Joan. "I really shouldn't be at all surprised if you're not making the proverbial mountain out of the legendary molehill. I'm sure the boy will say nothing."

"Aha!" I said. "So do you admit to fornicating with him?"

Joan smiled demurely. "Ask me no questions, I'll tell you no lies."

"This is quite simply outrageous," I said, sitting in my wing chair to still my trembling legs. "Joan, you may understand men, because Lord knows you've met enough of them in your time. But I can assure you that you do not understand boys. And Ralph Hotchkiss is still a boy. I have lived amongst adolescents all my life and I know whereof I speak. There are certain boys who will kiss and not tell, but they are rare creatures indeed and I do not number an amiable oaf such as Ralph Hotchkiss amongst them."

"Oh fiddlesticks," she said. "On Sunday we'll be in Mexico for a whole glorious week. When we return this will all be forgotten. It will just be another tempest in this damn teapot you call a school."

She went to the record player and put on something by one of her favourite composers, beastly Schoenberg. Joan had peculiar taste in music. On our wedding night she danced to Ravel's "Bolero," shedding her garments along the way. At the time I hadn't the heart to tell her that the insidious melodic line of that particular composition always tempted me to move my forefinger up and down my lips like an imbecile.

So, this Hotchkiss business took place on Friday night and the next afternoon found me on my way to the Land of Smiles, driving through pleasant wooded countryside. The snow glittered in the February sunlight. How strange that in this country of feverish yellow light I yearn for snow! The other day I suddenly began to repeat the lines of that beloved old Christian hymn "Good King Wenceslaus."

When the snow lay round about
Deep and crisp and even.

I wept at the familiar words I had so often sung at midnight carol service. And I was very close to tears as I drove toward the facility through that sunlit winter afternoon. Have I mentioned a previous breakdown? It happened during my first year at university when I became discouraged with classics and tried to switch to English literature. However, I was too late and the authorities refused my request. As a consequence I went into a spin that lasted several months. I have obviously inherited my father's nerves, and the notion of my career suddenly going up in smoke made them more than a little taut. I was glad I'd had the good sense to buy a bottle of Bristol Cream.

My aunts at once noticed my downcast state. "Whatever is the matter with our Philip today?" asked Aunty Fay as she placed a tray of biscuits on the coffee table. We were seated in their small comfortable apartment and I had just poured the sherry.

"I'm sorry," I said. "I don't wish to burden you." I raised my glass. "Cheers, Aunties."

"Let us," said Aunt Florence, "hear no further talk of burdens. Self-pity is not a Bannister trait, Philip." Aunty Flo is larger than her sister and rather majestic in both figure and manner. "No one is critical of your present arrangement, but marriage does not run in the family. Your sister and I had plenty of beaus, to be sure. Why, Fay went out with a defenceman for the New York Rangers the year they won the Stanley Cup. Nineteen and thirty-three. Do you remember, Fay? They had Andy Aitkenhead in goal. They called him the Glasgow Gobbler. And Fay dated a nice boy from northern Ontario, I think." Aunty Flo drank some sherry. "We used often to go to the old Gardens. And the fights at the St. Nicholas Arena. Do you remember that boy, Fay? A defenceman. He wanted to marry you. Out of the question, of course."

Aunty Fay blushed at the memory while her sister continued. "The truth is that we Bannisters are just too independent. We just don't like bringing other people into the family. It never works, somehow. You remember Cousin Agnes, Fay? And look what happened to her!" This was left. "And take your poor father, Philip! If your mother hadn't died giving birth to you, I'm not at all sure he could have tolerated living in the house with a perfect stranger. He only knew your mother a month before he married her, poor fellow. He did the honourable thing, of course, but I'm sure that over the long haul it wouldn't have worked. We Bannisters are not the marrying types and that seems to be that. Have another butter tart, dear boy, you look a bit fragile. How is the food these days at the school, by the way? Is the new chef working out?"

"As a matter of fact, no. There have been complaints."

"What a pity!"

"Oh, do let's play our new game," said Aunty Fay, filling her glass. She is a blithe little soul and never one for pursuing dreary subjects. "Join us, Philip, please. It's ever so much more fun with three."

My aunts and their games! How they filled my childhood with happiness! While my poor father gazed at his astrolabe or polished his napkin ring, my aunts played games with me. And unlike ordinary parents who feel obliged to spend a dutiful few minutes each evening with a child, my aunts would play for hours in the big house on Sparrow Hill Road. There were endless games of Up

Jenkins and Pinch Without Laughing. And Hide-and-Go-Seek amid the furniture of the large, drafty rooms that were once the servants' quarters on the third floor. I can still see Aunty Fay on her hands and knees as she disappeared with a gasp of delight behind a divan. And they are still at it! Now too elderly for the rigours of physical games, they still indulge their love of fancy and invention.

The latest of these diversions was called Least Favourites and was deceptively simple, comprising as it did the naming of one's least favourite whatever. I expected something exceptionally intricate, a chemical, say, or a synthetic. In fact, by way of introducing the game, they chose a simple item, namely a musical instrument. Taking another glass of sherry, Aunty Flo asked, "So now, dear Philip. What is your least favourite musical instrument?"

"Well now, let me see," I said with a frown meant to convey serious consideration. Of course, upon hearing the question I had known at once. "I would have to say the accordion, Aunty. It has never excited my admiration."

"An excellent choice," said Aunty Flo, snapping off a piece of the facility's provender. It looked very like a ship's biscuit, the hardtack of sea legend. Aunty Flo still has her original teeth, though they are brown and mostly wrecked.

"I totally concur," said Aunty Fay, looking stern at the mention of accordions. "The instrument makes quite an objectionable sound and is fit only for persons from remote regions who dress up in outlandish costume and caper about in some primitive manner." She leaned forward. "Second least favourite, Philip?"

The game ran to three choices and then another contestant was allowed to play. I've forgotten how they determined a winner. It was only a bit of innocent tomfoolery designed to lighten their afternoon and take my mind off the possibility that at that very moment, Ralph Hotchkiss (to account for his lacklustre play?) was telling his teammates between periods that he was tired (wiped out?) having spent the previous night "screwing old Bannister's wife silly. She loved it, guys, I'm telling ya. She couldn't get enough, etc., etc."

"Come, come, Philip," said Aunty Fay, taking more sherry. "We others would like a turn."

And so my destiny appeared to wait upon the discretion of an eighteen-year-old hockey player! Oh, it was monstrously unfair! "Well," I said. "As you both know, I love music. Many sorts, really, except of course that rock nonsense and vile Schoenberg. Joan likes Arnold Schoenberg's music. I really can't imagine why."

"The music of Arnold Schoenberg," said Aunty Flo tartly, "is not to be tolerated in polite company."

"I totally concur," said her sister, finishing her sherry.

"I thought," said Aunty Flo, "that your wife looked a little peaked the last time we saw her. That was Christmas, was it not? She didn't look at all well in my opinion."

Aunty Fay said, "There's been a great deal of influenza around this winter."

"I wasn't think of influenza, Fay. I had in mind something far more serious. Her colour was very poor indeed. Has she see George Rugg lately?"

"We don't use Rugg anymore, Aunty," I said. "Joan didn't care for his manner."

"His manner?" said Aunty Flo, straightening her shoulders. "Nonsense. His manner is perfectly adequate. He's a blunt man, to be sure, and I'm not entirely convinced that he is as attentive to the practice of medicine as perhaps one ought to be if one is a physician. For that I blame his excessive interest in the stock market. Certainly he's not as dedicated as his father, but he is capable of performing a routine examination. George Rugg knows what a tongue depressor looks like. The Ruggs have served the Bannisters for years. I didn't know young George was no longer your family physician, Philip. Who is *she* seeing, then? I'll have another splash of sherry, Fay."

I named our doctor, a handsome young man. The sherry bottle was nearly empty and I had yet to finish my first glass.

"Now," said Aunty Fay, smiling. "Second least favourite, Philip?"

"I don't know, Aunty," I said desperately. I felt ill at the thought of *l'affaire* Hotchkiss spreading like plague across the campus. I saw the headmaster's redoubtable eyebrows climbing his forehead. *"Bannister's wife and who?"*

"Philip, *please*," said Aunty Fay. "You must have a second least favourite musical instrument."

I said, "Well, the triangle, I suppose. It's a limited device at best and the sound produced is in no way remarkable."

"I'm not so sure," Aunty Fay said, "that the triangle can be considered a legitimate musical instrument."

"Of course it can," interrupted Aunty Flo. She sounded grumpy. "It most assuredly can be considered a legitimate musical instrument."

Aunty Fay had set her mouth firmly. "And what makes you so absolutely certain of that, Florence?"

"The triangle is a legitimate musical instrument, Fay," said Aunt Florence. "That is common knowledge."

"It isn't."

"It is."

"Isn't."

"Is."

I should, of course, never have allowed them access to so much sherry; I blame my distracted state. Even the gentlest and most good-natured soul can become choleric after too much drink. I knew, however, that within the hour both of them would be napping and awaken refreshed and conciliatory. Meantime, to deflect their mild quarrelling, I blurted out the news that Joan and I were going to Mexico the next day. I explained that I'd been allowed to add a few days to the midterm break and so we would be gone for a week.

"Mexico?" said Aunty Flo, looking grim. "We were there in the winter of twenty-nine. Do you remember, Fay?" She paused to pour the last of the sherry. "I can't imagine why you would want to go there. It's a hot and smelly place."

"I expect it's changed a little since you were there, Aunty. In any case, we're not going to the mainland but to an island off the Yucatán Peninsula. It's called Cozumel."

"Never heard of it," sniffed Aunty Flo.

Her sister patted my knee and with her other hand stifled a yawn. "Of course you must do what you think best, dear."

"I hope," said Aunt Flo, "that you will tell your wife to be careful. It's easy to have a nasty accident in those regions. The water may not be drunk, of course, containing, as it does, any amount of undesirable matter. And speaking of water, I would issue a warning about the sea. One thinks immediately of drowning or sharks. Fay, I'm sure you remember Rosalind Butterworth? She was, of course, Rosalind Bight before her marriage to Taffy Butterworth. Rosalind was a classmate of ours at St. Melody's. Pretty little thing but scatterbrained. She and Taffy took a holiday in Mexico. Oh, this was years ago! They went out one day on a fishing boat and the woman was devoured by sharks. Or, at any rate, some species of large, ravenous fish. Taffy said she fell off the boat, though some say he pushed her. No way of knowing, of course, and the Mexican authorities are, I understand, rather lax about these matters. In general I would hazard the opinion that the Latins are not a reliable people. Certainly that fishing-boat business was very rum. Taffy went on to marry the cement heiress. What was her name, Fay? Heavens, it was a household word! Oh, Fay, do wake up! This is most unseemly with Philip visiting."

Oh, my dear aunts! How I miss you here in this country of feverish yellow light where I am eating a mango and reading the opening pages of *The Moonstone*. "I address these lines—written in India—to my relatives in England. My object is to explain the motive which has induced me to refuse the right hand of friendship to my cousin John Herncastle." How I long to be reading those familiar lines to my students while the light of a winter afternoon wanes, and tea and buns await me in the Common Room. And later an evening of house duty where *in loco parentis* I could deal with the problems of young boys far from home. How could I have thought they were such nuisances? How could I have become so enraged when a student rang my doorbell late at night to ask for a piece of string? I reflect on my rudeness to poor Arthur Clegg. I am sorry, Arthur, wherever you are. There is surely a valuable lesson to be learned here. In the mundane we must find our contentment or perish unsatisfied, for the dramatic life is an unhappy life. Murderers and other celebrities know this only too well.

Nine

Please forgive a foolish old maniac for straying from his narrative with the foregoing reminiscences, but I have been suffering of late from headaches which punish and bewilder my brain. Where was I in this chronicle of woe? Looking back I see I have already recounted how the weirdly amiable Ted Hacker tried to drown me before offering *his* hand in friendship. I was badly shaken by that experience and furious with Joan, who refused to believe that my life had been threatened. To her it was all some enormous joke that I had failed to appreciate. As a consequence we retired that evening without speaking.

The next morning I awakened to voices and laughter from the swimming pool below our balcony. Before I opened my eyes I could smell coffee. This struck me as peculiar since I could not remember having arranged for breakfast to be delivered to our room. When I opened my eyes, however, I beheld Corky Hacker standing by the dresser pouring coffee. She looked fresh and lovely in sandals, snug white jeans and a striped jersey, the very image of a wealthy yachtsman's companion. Joan was nowhere to be seen. Looking over at me, Corky Hacker smiled and said, "Well, it's about time you rose and shone, Philip Bannister." She came across the room bearing a cup of coffee. "I thought you might like some breakfast."

I am not used to facing strange women first thing in the morning and I felt acutely uncomfortable. The awakening person always feels vulnerable in front of someone who has been up and about for a time. My mouth was sour and my bowels were full; in fact, I prefer to be left alone for the first twenty minutes of the day.

"May I ask what you are doing here?" I said. "And where is my wife?" Corky Hacker sat down on the bed. There was amusement in her light grey eyes. She smelled of soap and fresh lemon.

"Joan says you're not a heavy breakfast person, so I just ordered some melon, toast and coffee, though I recommend the *huevos rancheros*. Ted and I had them this morning and they're wonderful." She handed me the coffee.

"Where is Joan?" I asked, sitting up. "And what time is it?"

"It's nearly ten," she said. "And Joanie's gone into the village with Ted. He wants to rent one of those funny little cars. You know, the ones that look like big baby carriages. He thought it would be nice if we went on a picnic. Joan and I think it's a great idea, too. Ted's arranged everything. The hotel is packing a picnic hamper for us. Ted thinks maybe we could explore the other end of the island."

"Ted does, does he?"

But Corky Hacker took no notice of my tone. There seemed to be a total absence of irony in her nature. "How's the coffee?" she asked.

"Look," I said. "You'll have to count me out of this picnic business."

She affected surprise. "But why, Philip? It'll be fun."

"This is incredible," I said, placing my cup of coffee on the table beside my bed. "Just what makes you think I want to go on a picnic with your husband? After what he . . ."

Corky Hacker laughed. "But Joan and I will be going along too, silly."

The coffee sat on my empty stomach like lye. "This is ludicrous," I said, settling myself into a more comfortable position. "Now please listen to me. I have nothing personal against you, Mrs. Hacker."

"Oh, Corky, please," she interrupted.

"Well, Corky then. And as I say, I have nothing personal against you. In fact," I hesitated, "I like you. But at the same time I have to confess that I just don't care for your husband. I'm sorry but that's the way it is. I don't understand his sense of humour. If that's what you call it."

Corky Hacker smiled and placed a hand on my arm. "Oh, Philip, please don't take Ted so seriously. He's really a very nice guy. Maybe he gets a little enthusiastic but that's just his way. He's a naturally exuberant person and full of *joie de vivre*. That's what makes him such a great salesman. And he just loves people. He really likes you, Philip. Do you know what he said to me last night?"

"How could I know that?" I asked miserably.

"Last night we were lying in bed talking over the day and what fun we'd had. Especially after we met you and Joanie. And Ted said to me, 'Cork. That Philip Bannister is a real gentleman.' He said that to me, Philip, so help me Hannah!"

"That's wonderful," I said, "but he also nearly

drowned me last night. Forgive my saying so, but your husband is a physical bully."

"Oh, I'm sure he didn't mean it," said Corky. "Ted wouldn't hurt a fly. In nine years of marriage he hasn't laid a hand on me and believe you me I've given him reason. I can be darn hard to get along with, really temperamental. But not once has Ted come even close to abuse. Gosh, Ted's a Big Brother, Philip. The boys love him. He takes them to football and basketball games. He buys them ice cream." She smiled sadly. "We can't have children. Ted had mumps as a child and they settled in his stones. We're still thinking about adopting."

In his stones. That curious phrase had a strange effect upon me. I stirred as Corky Hacker laid a cool hand against my brow. "You look a little pale this morning. Are you feeling all right?"

"Just a mild hangover." I felt like a child as she placed the back of her hand against my cheek.

"Poor Philip."

"Why 'poor Philip'?"

She brightened. "How about some melon? It's very good."

"I'm sure it is," I said, adding, "My wife and your husband seem to be awfully chummy on very short acquaintance."

Corky Hacker laughed and I saw her pink tongue and small perfect teeth. "Are you jealous, Philip?"

"Not particularly."

"You strike me as the jealous type. Quiet and brooding." She studied my face. "I don't mind a streak of jealousy in a man. I like *intense* men."

From beyond the window came the voice of Fred Flintstone, who was loudly wagering with a companion over the outcome of a race in the swimming pool. "What you've got to understand, Philip," said Corky Hacker, "is that Ted's a natural flirt. It goes with his extroverted personality. All the women doctors and pharmacists get a kick out of him. You should have heard them talking about Ted and how his visits cheer them up. Several of them told me this last October at the pharmaceutical convention in Omaha. But it's all kidding around. Ted's never been unfaithful to me."

"How can you be so sure?" I asked, watching her trim little behind as she walked across the room to the breakfast tray.

She returned with a dish of melon. Sitting on the bed she said, "Now I'm going to feed you some of this nice melon, so open up." Like an invalid I opened my mouth to receive the cool fruit.

While Corky Hacker fed me, I listened to the voices and laughter from the pool, and watched the sunlight playing along the walls. From time to time our eyes met. In this fresh-smelling housewife from the plains of America I detected a promise of rich sensuality. I saw her in a summer dress among her shiny appliances, or sitting naked on the commode to shave her legs or underarms. As she fed me she said, "If anyone's been tempted it's been me."

"Tempted?" I asked.

"Oh yes," she said. "You'd be surprised at what goes on in my mind!"

"What makes you say that?"

She looked away. "Well, maybe you wouldn't. I'll bet

behind all that refinement and blue-blazer stuff, Philip Bannister knows the score." I said nothing to that. "I have a pretty dirty mind, I guess," said Corky Hacker, blushing. "I wrote this story once. I was taking a night course in creative writing at the university. It was just something to do with Ted away so much. And I thought I would just write some romantic stuff, but everything I wrote came out kind of sexy." She suddenly laughed and covered her mouth with a hand. "I really shocked the instructor with this one story."

"Really?"

"Yes. He asked me to stay after class. Then he made a pass at me." Corky fed herself some melon. "Actually it was more than a pass. He ripped my dress. He was in a frenzy. He said he was prepared to give up his wife and kids for me. He got down on his knees and started to cry like a baby. It was kind of crazy."

"I'm not surprised," I said, placing my small oar carefully into the water. "You're a very attractive woman."

"Oh, there were lots of women prettier than me in that class, Philip. But I think my story turned him on."

"Perhaps," I said, wincing at that ugly and obsolete phrase. Did they still use such terminology in the American corn belt?

"I was tempted to sleep with him," she said. "Maybe just once to see what he was like. He was awfully good-looking. That's why there were so many women in his class, I guess. But I resisted temptation. Wasn't I a good little girl?" she added, smiling and spooning the last of the fruit into my mouth.

"That must have been some story," I said.

"Oh gosh, yes. I hid it in the cedar chest in case Ted got

hold of it. Ted is a very moral person. He's always going on about the smut merchants, as he calls them. He's a bit nutty on the subject."

"I'm sure your story was not mere smut."

"Well, I didn't think so. I mean, I thought it was kind of artistic the way I did it. This creative-writing instructor said it was good enough to be published in some magazine in New York. *Playgirl* or something. But maybe he was just saying that to get in my pants. And anyway, I kept thinking, what would happen if people I know found out about it. Like all our friends at the Okey-Dokey Club and the church. Not to mention Ted or his parents. Gosh, I'll bet the last book Mom Hacker read was *The Big Fisherman* or something like that."

"People take these things more in their stride nowadays," I said. "You may have anticipated too much."

"Oh, I'm not so sure about that, Philip. You have to live in Lincoln to understand how straight it is."

The adorable woman had absently placed a hand on my thigh; it rested there, a few miserly centimetres from my morning erection. She shook her nest of tight curls. "No sir. Polly has to stay in the cedar chest or my marriage could go ka-pow!"

"Polly?" I asked.

"Yes. That's the title of my story. And I guess if it were published, everybody would wonder if I'm like her. See, Polly has all these lovers. It starts out one perfectly ordinary Monday morning when she's doing the washing in her basement. She has just put in a load of dark clothes when this terrific-looking guy from the gas company comes down to read the meter. Right away there's a kind of chemistry between them and Polly finds herself saying why not. It's like they realize they are destined to share this moment of intimacy. So he unzips her jeans and pulls down her panties and he gives it to her right there standing up against the laundry tubs. And right away, bang, bang, bang, she has these three terrific orgasms all in a row. She nearly *faints*."

"Ah."

"See, she's excited by the danger, too, because at that moment her husband is upstairs shaving and her two little kids are eating their Cheerios in the kitchen."

With her mind cast adrift in her story, Corky Hacker looked away and then innocently lifted her hand from my leg to rub an itch under her nose. "After that, Polly figures she'll really have a good time. So she becomes involved with this Greek restaurant owner. Then there's her doctor who is Japanese. And a handsome young Filipino who comes to fix the Lawn-Boy."

"And how does it all end?" I asked, as her butterfly of a hand alighted once more on my thigh.

"Well, Polly tires of it all. She sees the error of her ways. She loses her husband and her children, but then she's saved by this dynamite television evangelist."

"Well, I don't think you have anything to worry about," I said. "Such a story should satisfy even the good citizens of Lincoln, Nebraska. What you have constructed, in fact, is the perfect morality tale. Your character has a great deal of fun, but is made to suffer for it and finds redemption in the end. People have made fortunes out of such stories."

Corky Hacker grinned at me. "Gee, I hadn't thought of it that way, Philip." Was it my imagination or was her hand actually squeezing my leg? "Gosh, I'm glad we had this talk," she said. "It's so nice to talk to someone who *understands*. Please don't get me wrong. Ted is a great guy and I love him. He's a wonderful man. But he just doesn't understand these kinds of things."

We looked carefully at one another and for a moment I thought we might embrace; indeed, I grasped her wrists, preparing to seize the hour and commit my first act of adultery. But with surprising swiftness for one so slim, Corky Hacker loosened my grip and stood up. "Well, I guess Ted and Joanie will soon be getting back. I'm going to my room to get into my bathing suit." Poking a finger into my ribs she said sternly, "Come on now, Mr. B. Time to get up! The day is already half gone."

After she left, the tumescent old hog lay in bed listening to other tourists at play. I heard the diving board resound mightily as Fred (The Human Cannonball) Flintstone issued a terrible directive to all in his path. "Yabba-dabba-do," yelled Fred on his descent.

Ten

To keep peace in the family I went on the picnic. Both my wife and Ted Hacker kept inquiring about my headache, and in the rear seat of the absurd little car he had rented, Joan rested her head against my shoulder like a foolish teenager. My suspicions were at once aroused. Without fail the cuckold becomes an object of pity and concern in the eyes of the transgressors. Husbands, beware of those ordinary Monday evenings when the little woman announces that instead of leftover pot roast, there will be lamb provençale and a bottle of Chateau Bliss. Before you take a bite, ask if there have been male visitors to your house that afternoon: a real estate agent, a college student selling magazine subscriptions, the handsome gas meter man (à la Corky Hacker's story)? Wives, regard with scepticism the flowers he hands you in the hallway. Susy Secretary may still be sighing from her boss's ministrations. Living with a woman who was chronically unfaithful had, of course, made me more sensitive about such matters. In this particular instance, I could not be certain and it was pointless to ask Joan. For her, everything quickly assumed the dimensions of an enormous joke.

To give Hacker his due, he had arranged everything from the car to the lunch and the beer. He had also rented some equipment for inspecting fish, a pastime that held no interest for me. I had brought along some more duty reading: an "overview" of Canadian poetry and fiction (*A Nation's Larynx)* written by some fellow who teaches in a university in Alberta. I noticed that there was extensive coverage of Dwight Tushy's flummery.

We had soon passed several large hotels south of the village and were skimming along the road by the sea. On the other side of the highway lay the jungle. Hacker stopped the car alongside a promising stretch of beach and we unloaded the supplies. Corky Hacker seemed greatly amused by the high spirits of her husband and my wife, but Joan's gaiety was getting on my nerves. Sometimes, when she is in a fiercely good humour, she will affect some hideous accent. Her involvement in amateur theatre convinced her that she possessed gifts of mimicry. That wretched Don Whipple once assigned her the part of Mrs. Gogan in *The Plough and the Stars*, and from time to time I am made to suffer a stage Irish accent. So, as Joan in shorts and halter handed me a cold bottle of Carta Blanca, she said, "Here you go, then, me boyo!" The Hackers were spreading a blanket on the sand. From under her large straw hat Joan winked at me. "How's the beer, me darlin' boy? Is it after suitin' ya?"

"That will do, Joan," I said. "That will be just about enough of that kind of talk." She laughed and I gazed at her large pale knees. Had horrible Hacker been burrowing between them only hours before? The man in question walked over to us. He was wearing a floral shirt and a pair of wide yellow pants with an elasticized waistband.

"What do you say to a dip before lunch, kiddo?" he said to Joan and lightly slapped her backside.

"Maybe yes, maybe no," Joan said coyly.

Hacker suddenly looked grim. "Well, take a walk, then.

Corky will go with you. I want a word with Phil here."

"Okay, Ted," said Joan. I was amazed, for Joan was not the type to take orders. But she walked toward the shore where Corky Hacker was already bent over studying something underfoot.

Hacker and I sat down on the blanket and, sipping our beer, watched my wife's slow walk through the sand. "You're a very lucky man, Phil," he said. "That's a lot of lovely woman you've got there, amigo." He continued to stare at Joan and then said, "What do you think of *my* wife?"

"What do you mean, what do I think of her?"

Hacker was now leaning back on his elbows. He looked sideways at me. "Well," he said, "do you think she's good-looking?" He sounded aggrieved, even petulant. I found his question strange and his manner peculiar and so I hesitated. He had put on a pair of those mirror sunglasses that do not permit you even a glimpse of the person's eyes. In fact, looking over at him I saw in those sinister-looking spectacles only my own small, distorted self.

"Well, come on, fellah," Hacker said. "I asked you a question."

"Well, yes," I said. "She is indeed very good-looking."

"You better believe it, buddy," said Hacker, abruptly shifting his gaze toward the two women who were now walking along the shore. They were obviously conversing and Corky Hacker was using her hands a great deal to explain something or other. "The Cork used to be a drum majorette," said Hacker, his eyes following the women's progress along the beach.

"Is that so?"

"Yes, that is so," he said, looking over at me again with his weird glasses. "I've got a picture of her."

"You keep a picture of your wife as a high-school drum majorette?"

"No, no, no," he said, shaking his large head, "not high school. College. She was a drum majorette for the Cornhuskers' band." He leaned over and extracted from his pocket a fat wallet. From this he produced a snapshot of his wife. And there indeed was Corky Hacker at nineteen or so; captured forever on some October afternoon in Nebraska. She looked saucy and lewd in her drum majorette costume.

"Very nice," I said, handing back the photograph. Hacker carefully returned it to his wallet and then, propped on elbows, looked again at the diminishing figures of the two women. I sipped some Carta Blanca and leafed through the unsatisfactory volume on my country's literature.

After a moment Hacker asked, "So how long have you and Joanie been married, Phil?"

"It will be three years in October," I said.

"Is that a fact?"

"It's a fact."

Hacker sighed. "The Cork and I have been married for nearly ten years. We'll be celebrating our tenth anniversary in June."

"How nice for you!"

He looked over at me. "You don't have to be sarcastic, Phil. You don't have to knock the pins out from under someone who is just trying to be friendly."

"Now wait just a minute."

"No, you wait just a minute," he said. He rolled onto

his stomach. "That phrase of yours 'How nice for you' was just dripping with sarcasm. You're not interested in other people at all, are you, Phil? I don't know how you can even call yourself a teacher. Are you teachers not the guardians of learning? Do you not pass on the burning torch of knowledge to the young? I'll bet you don't, you conceited little poop."

"Now listen, Hacker!"

Shifting his large restless body he returned to lean on his elbows and look out to sea. He shook his head. "You're a heartless old devil, Phil."

"Well, why not just ignore me?" I asked, picking up my book. "You don't have to put up with me," I continued angrily. "After all, I was practically dragged to this damn picnic. I would have been equally content back at the hotel by the swimming pool."

Hacker snapped off his glasses and sat up. His blue eyes looked so wild that I was afraid he might strike me. "Hey, just a minute," he cried. "Can't you take a little honest criticism? I *like* you, darn it. And so does Cork." He returned the sunglasses to his face and leaned back. The women were now returning, Corky Hacker's arms still flailing in the air. Both of us watched the shore and said nothing. A bitter silence seemed to envelop us; I could no longer concentrate on my book. The air appeared to be freighted with menace. It was as though I was entangled in Hacker's oddly shifting mood, and again I wondered if he were mad. Perhaps he was a schizophrenic? How were they supposed to behave? Did any two behave alike? I knew little of psychiatry and was inclined to regard its practice as more claptrap from a demented century.

Earlier Hacker had removed his shoes and stockings. Now he began to knock his long white feet together. At the same time he made objectionable clicking sounds with his teeth and tongue. Deriving any sense from the words before my eyes was out of the question. Finally Hacker said, "Corky and I were both virgins on our wedding night."

"Really?" I said, looking up from my book. Had I heard the man correctly? The day had grown overcast and in the heavy grey air the flies were abundant. One settled on Hacker's yellow pants and he flattened the life from it with a smack of his palm.

"How about you and Joan?" he asked.

I laughed hollowly. "Good heavens, man, Joan was married twice before she met me."

"I thought as much," Hacker said, looking down at his damn feet which he continued to knock together.

I put aside my book. "And just what do you mean by that?"

"Oh, I don't know, Phil," he said. "She just strikes me as a woman of experience, that's all. It's just an observation."

"Well, of course, we're both much older than you," I said.

"Oh, I don't think age has anything to do with it at all," said Hacker sententiously.

What on earth was going through his mind? I wondered. Was he subjecting me to a subtle form of torment? Looking at his profile, the blond hair damp with humidity, the blank glasses, the handsome nose and mouth, I felt a richly satisfying anger. I saw exactly where the bullet would enter the temple. After several hours, only the puckered skin and the faint blue stain would mark its passage. The calibre had been small but lethal. Manufactured in France, the model was not as yet available to agents in the Middle East and other trouble spots.

"How many times a week," Hacker asked, "do you and Joan have intercourse?"

"What business is that of yours?" I asked irritably.

"Oh, come on, Phil," said Hacker, sitting up and pushing the glasses onto his hair. He raised his knees and laced his hands over them. "We'll probably never meet again. What's the diff? We're just tourists on vacation. Strangers who pass one another and are seen no more. It's a well-known observation that people say things to strangers that they wouldn't dream of saying to their best friends. And why not? It's a great opportunity to get things off the old chest. It's one of the advantages of travel. You'd be surprised at what people tell me when I'm travelling. Allow me to assure you that in airplanes and hotel bars, I get a mighty earful. Why, a fellow last month! We were snowed in somewhere. Minneapolis, as a matter of fact. We were snowed in and sitting in the airport bar. Just a couple of salesmen shooting the breeze. And do you know what this guy told me?"

"What?"

Absurdly Hacker looked around as though we were in a crowded room and he wished to unveil a confidence. He dropped his voice. "He told me that the only thing that turns him and his wife on is peanut butter and strawberry jam." Hacker grinned and shook his head, amazed and delighted at the revelations of his fellow creatures. "See, what this guy told me is that his wife spreads crunchy peanut butter on his . . . his *thing*, for crying out loud. Isn't that something? And he in turn puts strawberry jam on her . . . you know, her *muff*. Can you beat that? I mean, that strikes me as very strange behaviour."

"Oh, I don't know about that," I said, feigning a yawn. I was not about to appear impressed by his Minneapolis nonsense. In any case, I had heard, even in my own narrow world, of far more eccentric sexual habits. "What those people were doing," I said, "was reverting to childhood appetites. Both of them are obviously fixated on childhood. They were, you see, not so much interested in sex, which is, after all, an adult pleasure, but in merely consuming a peanut butter and jam sandwich, which is more within the pleasure range of children. Or people who still behave like children." I was enjoying the look of puzzled interest on Hacker's face. "For my part," I continued, "I would have been more impressed with your Minneapolis salesman and his good lady if they had used beluga caviar and Mumm's."

Hacker's face again broke into a wide grin and he delivered a stinging blow to my arm. "You know something, Phil? You're quite the card. Beluga caviar and Mumm's! That's pretty good. I'll bet behind that private-school stuff you're quite a character."

"I am not without my amusing side," I said, reaching for another bottle of beer.

"And I'll bet you're a horny little terror too," said Hacker, chuckling.

I was ready for this; I was not going to be intimidated by this behemoth from the plains of America. "So how many times," I asked, "do you and *your* wife? In a week, I mean?"

Hacker brushed away the flies from his feet and gave

me a curious sidelong glance. "How's that, Phil?"

"As you said before, we shall probably never see one another again after this week. These are harmless disclosures and quickly forgotten when one returns to the workaday world."

"Our sex life," announced Hacker, "is mutually satisfying."

"Of course. I never suggested otherwise."

"Ho ho. And you'd better not if you know what's good for you." We again fell into an uneasy silence. The women were still several hundred yards away and they had stopped to examine something by the water's edge. I wondered what *they* were talking about.

The beer and the heat of the Mexican noon stunned my will and left me languid. The windless, grey day seemed oppressive and the flies never ceased buzzing about our heads. I almost forgot Ted Hacker. I watched a cruise ship moving slowly along the horizon and thought about my colleagues now sitting down to lunch in Bung Hall. Today was Monday and so they would be served boiled potatoes and stiff blackened ovals of ground meat. The boys referred to them as hockey pucks and sometimes used them in pickup games behind Knock House. This led me to speculate on what the hotel had prepared for our lunch, and I wondered indeed if anything edible could be enjoyed in the midst of the heat and the flies. These thoughts were interrupted by Hacker, who leaned toward me. "Tell me, Phil," he said, "do you ever get a little restless?"

"Restless?" I repeated. The foolish man looked worried and vulnerable as he stroked his great flat cheeks. I decided to torment him a little. "How do you mean 'restless'?"

He grimaced and showed me his teeth. "Oh come on, buddy. You know what I mean."

"No, I'm afraid I don't."

He looked away to the lead-coloured sea. "Oh come on, Phil. You know what I'm getting at. A little bite of forbidden fruit. A taste of something different."

"Are you asking me whether I ever contemplate intercourse with a woman other than my wife?"

"That's about the size of it, yes."

I sipped some more beer. Hacker looked so pathetically eager that I felt as though I were back in my classroom counselling some boy who was suffering through the endless anxieties of adolescence.

"Well, I suppose it's only natural," I said. "But you must bear in mind that at a boarding school there is little opportunity for philandering. During term we schoolmasters are too busy to be unfaithful. I believe idleness promotes fornication, and we have little time on our hands with lessons and games and whatnot. I suppose," I added, "it must be quite different for a salesman."

Hacker gloomily surveyed the grey sea and said nothing. I recalled Corky Hacker's comment on her husband's faithfulness. Was she right? I wondered. Few men like to be congratulated on being stodgily true for ten years. "Being on the move the way you are," I said, "it's certainly to your credit that during all those years of marriage you haven't strayed."

"Who says I haven't?" Hacker grunted.

"Well, I just assumed, I suppose . . ."

"Don't assume anything, Phil."

"Of course. I was merely . . ."

"Say a word to my wife and I'll break your arm. I'll snap it like a dry twig. Make it look like an accident." He was now staring at me with his wild blue eyes. "I can do it, too, Phil. I've got my black belt in karate. I was also in the marines. I learned how to kill men with my bare hands. I know the nine major pressure points of the human body."

I could summon no fitting response to such talk and so remained silent.

Hacker picked up a handful of sand and watched the grains sift through his fingers. "Gosh, I just *hate* a snitcher," he said. The women were now coming up from the shore and I was glad to see them, for my bizarre companion unnerved me.

To change the subject I suggested that we lay out the lunch. "We could have things ready for the ladies," I said.

"Good idea," said Hacker, getting up and dusting the sand from the seat of his pants. He looked thoughtful as he watched the approach of our wives.

"Maybe one of these nights, Phil," he said, "you and I could leave the girls at the hotel and go into town. See what the local action looks like. Get us a little poontang!"

Eleven

Lunch was not a success. We ate little and in silence. A melancholy seemed to have overtaken the entire outing. The fruit and beer and sandwiches quickly surrendered to the heat, and the flies covered everything. A few yards from the blanket and behind a piece of driftwood, Joan discovered the decaying corpse of a large seabird. When a few drops of warm rain began to fall, Corky Hacker sighed and touched her husband's arm. "I think it's going to rain, Teddy. Maybe we should go back to the hotel." A brooding Hacker stared at the ground between his legs.

"That's a very good idea," I said.

Joan laid a hand on Hacker's arm. "Ted, it was a perfectly charming idea. None of this is your fault."

Corky Hacker placed her slender arms around her husband's neck and pressed her face against his. "Don't be blue, big Teddy bear," she whispered. "We'll go back to the hotel and have some fun?" Drawing back she cocked her frizzy head to one side like a bird. "Come on now," she said. "We'll do the Monkey Trick if you like."

"What on earth is the Monkey Trick?" I asked.

Hacker raised his great head to glare at me. "None of your damn business, Bannister." I was startled, too, by his wife's malevolent look. Hacker arose, waving angrily at the flies. "He's probably glad it's going to rain."

He was right, of course, though I strenuously denied it.

More fat drops were now spattering the sand. "He's just glad, that's all," said Hacker, shaking out the blanket. He seemed ready to weep. Gathering up the picnic materials, we headed for the car. To placate Hacker, the women walked on either side of him, each holding an arm.

In the car Hacker looked glum and murderous as the rain fell harder across the highway. He drove quickly and we soon passed bicycles and motor scooters whose riders were soaked to the skin. We, too, were getting wet, though I didn't mind; the warm rain left me exhilarated. I suppose we always imagine a tropical country in sunlight, so it is not surprising that such a landscape looks peculiarly forlorn on a grey rainy day. Forlorn to some, that is. It looked fine to me, but then I enjoy the rain. I should have lived in England where the skies are often grey. How I used to enjoy the cloudbursts that interrupted a match! My hosts would serve me a cup of tea, and, sitting in the belvedere overlooking the pitch, I would watch the rain soaking the grass. Now whizzing along the wet Mexican highway in the little open car I felt nearly happy. Within the hour I would be in my dressing gown and reading a good mystery novel. No more "overview" of Canadian literature; I would spend the rest of the day with a thumping good read.

In this jaunty humour I glanced sideways at Joan. Her straw hat was obviously cheap stuff, for the rain had already weakened the fibres and caused the crown to sag. The whole affair had settled on her head like some large overturned nest. I thought the effect was quite comical and told her so.

"Oh, do shut up, Philip," she said without looking at me.

"As you wish, my dear," I replied. "Only trying to make conversation." I added "me darlin' girl" but I don't think she heard me.

In San Miguel the streets were mostly empty. In doorways tourists held shopping bags over their heads and waited for taxis. The restaurants had closed for the afternoon. When we reached the El Gringo Hotel, Hacker was the first to leave the car. We followed him as he splashed through puddles to reach the front door of the hotel. The desk clerk in the deserted lobby looked up from his newspaper to observe our arrival. He was a thin, consumptive-looking man with an unhappy face. "The rain," said this knight of mournful countenance, "is most unfortunate. And I would add most unusual for this time of year." He shrugged. "It probably will not last, my dear friends."

"It better not," said Hacker, standing arms akimbo in his colourful sodden clothes. "The travel agent back home told us it doesn't rain down here this time of year. I didn't spend good money to come down here and get rained on, darn it."

"Of course you didn't," said the clerk, returning to his newspaper. He appeared to have lost interest in the subject. Hacker charged up the short stairway to his room, followed by his wife.

As Joan and I walked to our room I said, "What an absurd fuss over a little rain! As if it were the poor clerk's fault!"

At once Joan turned to me and said angrily, "Oh, what do you know about it, Philip? What do you know about anything?"

In the room we undressed without speaking. I put on

my bathrobe and, though it was early in the day for whiskey, poured myself a generous measure, reasoning that I might easily have picked up a cold in my damp clothes. Returning from Mexico with a cold would have been preposterous; I would be the laughingstock of the Common Room. While I prepared the drink, my naked wife strode about the room with a cigarette in her mouth. As she paced back and forth, she dried her hair with a towel. Stopping by the balcony door she looked beyond the coconut palms to the grey sea. "Well, at least it's a good thing we didn't go across to Tulum today," she said.

"Oh," said I. "Were we supposed to?"

"Yes. Ted thought it would be a good idea. But we got up too late to catch the ferry. Don't you remember his mentioning it last night?"

"As a matter of fact, I don't."

"Well, of course, you were rather tight, weren't you?"

"Yes, I suppose I was. And justifiably so after escaping death at the hands of that madman."

"Oh, you're still on about that, are you?"

"Indeed, yes. One doesn't nearly get drowned every night of the week."

"Oh rubbish!" said Joan. "You exaggerate everything, Philip. And you have no sense of humour. I don't mind saying I've always resented that in you. Ted Hacker is a wonderful, warm human being and it's sheer nonsense to imagine he would harm anyone."

She sat on a chair with her legs apart and her head between her knees. With the towel she vigorously scrubbed her hair. I looked at the corns on her long toes and was filled with revulsion. Yet I was fascinated by her anger. For all of Joan's faults, and they were considerable, she possessed this remarkably amiable nature and it took a very great deal to get under her skin. This indeed was the angriest I had ever seen her, and I could not help but wonder why. Had the rain interrupted something more than just a picnic? Had the three of them been looking forward to something beyond the simple ingestion of victuals on a beach? And if so, why had I not been apprised of their plans? Certainly they were now all behaving like furious disappointed children. And Joan's rare ill humour had taken me aback. Someone who becomes angry only occasionally is more to be reckoned with than an habitually irascible person. Years of classroom experience, however, have provided me with skills appropriate for dealing with people who are "upset." The best method is by far to adopt a jaunty manner. And so, addressing my wife's towelled head, I said, "It was good of Hacker to organize our holidays for us. But I would just as leave we did things on our own. Naturally I assumed that you and I might visit the historic ruins of Tulum one day this week. The glories of the Mayan civilization and all that stuff. Perhaps we could have a little picnic of our own over there. When it isn't raining, of course."

Joan stopped towelling her head and gave me a bitter look. "Oh, you do carry on, don't you! I daresay if everything were left to you, we should all just sit around and *read*." Her voice was laden with contempt.

"Well," I said lightly, "sitting around reading happens to be my idea of a holiday, dear lady. And please don't use the phrase 'I daresay.' It makes you sound like one of those twits on *Masterpiece Theatre*."

"I never thought," Joan said, rather grandly, "that I should see the day, Philip, when I should have to call you a Canadian bumpkin. But the day seems to have arrived. You are a Canadian bumpkin."

"I most certainly reject that judgment," I said. It wasn't often that I could get to her like this; I was enjoying myself immensely. "If, as you say, I am a bumpkin, I wonder what an objective observer with some taste would make of our fellow tourist, the pill salesman from Lincoln, Nebraska."

"Don't you dare say another word about Ted Hacker," said Joan furiously.

I watched her walk to the bathroom and wondered what Hacker had done to inspire such loyalty. But I had no intention of leaving well enough alone, and so I called after her, "The both of you took your time this morning going into town. Two hours seems a very long time to arrange the rental of a car."

I walked to the open bathroom door. Joan was standing in front of the mirror pulling a brush through her hair. "We did some sightseeing."

"And what, pray, did you see?" I asked.

"Nothing terribly interesting, though Ted made it seem so. He's such an amusing man."

"Indeed," said I.

She looked at me and laughed. She was quickly regaining her good humour, a bad sign. I had hoped to keep her off guard a bit longer.

"Philip," she said, "you sound just like the jealous husband in some potty old play. I should have thought by now that you would have grown accustomed to things as they are." *I should have thought.* She tugged away at her thick matted hair. "Did you, by the way, like Corky?"

"*Did* I like her?"

"Sorry. Slip of the tongue. Do you like her?"

"What did you mean by 'did I like her?' Am I to interpret that in the sense of did I enjoy her? What the devil is going on around here, Joan? Am I supposed to have been up to something with Corky Hacker?" And if it had been so arranged, had I missed the opportunity of a lifetime? Oh, Bannister, you innocent fool!

Joan was now admiring her body. She placed her hands under her breasts. "Do you think my breasts are too large, Philip?"

"Yes."

"Corky Hacker is such a neat and trim little person, isn't she? Of course, she's ten years younger than I. And then, I have such a large frame."

She turned slowly to study her backside, which as a matter of fact was growing large and dimpled. Looking over her shoulder she winked at me. "But I think I've aged rather better than most, don't you, precious?"

"When we return home," I said, "I'm going to divorce you, Joan." This statement surprised me more than it did her. I had thought of divorce from time to time but was always repelled by the fuss and disorder that must attend such proceedings. I hadn't thought I would ever utter such a statement.

Joan, however, was not about to take me seriously, and as she left the bathroom she patted my cheek. "Nonsense, dear boy. There has never been a divorce at The Gannymede. It would be absolutely unheard of. And what would your dear old aunties think?"

"Applaud probably," I said, following her to the bed

where she lay down on her back. "They're not nearly as straightlaced as you imagine."

"Perhaps not," said Joan, raising one leg and then the other in some foolish calisthenic. "But I think we're much better off married. So I shan't give you a divorce."

"Oh, you shan't , shan't you?" I said, hoping to infuse her silly locution with irony. But she took no notice and continued to lift her legs.

"No, I shan't," she said.

"Then I shall very likely murder you," I said, standing over her.

Joan laughed. "My own absurd Philip. What a card you are! Come and lie down beside me." Her legs were now opening and closing like a pair of large pliers. Evidently she was again ready for intercourse, though I suppose that should not be thought of as so unusual. Many women, or so I have read, are receptive to insertions at least forty times a day. There was a prostitute in Hamburg, Germany, who was on record as having received vaginally two hundred male organs within twenty-four hours. I don't for a moment believe it, but one never knows about these matters.

But in the El Gringo Hotel that afternoon, I myself felt like intercourse. Ironically the dismal day had inspired an air of *volupté*; the memory of Corky Hacker's lemony smell as she spooned melon into me and the grey soft afternoon itself—they all engendered lewdness. Casting aside my dressing gown, I fell upon my wife's abundant flesh.

"My darling," laughed Joan as we embraced. "Shall we be mere missionaries or wild little people in the bushes?"

"Let us," said I, "venture into the bushes."
"Something a little outré, perhaps," said Joan.
"Why not?" I said.

There followed some erotic scuffling which I shall not bother to describe, as I have no interest in pandering to deviant mentalities. In the deplorable language of the police blotter, I was about to effect entrance when there came a loud and terrible rapping on our door. It was that most horrible of all announcements; the knuckled message of familiarity and bonhomie that so disheartens the sensitive amongst us, consisting as it did of seven raps on the wood, the first five maniacally fast followed by a pause before the last two, the entire performance adhering to the rhythmical structure of that old jingle "shave and a hair cut, two bits."

Joan fled to the bathroom while I put on my dressing gown. Upon opening the door I saw Corky Hacker in a white terry cloth outfit. There were sandals on her pretty feet and her hair was freshly brushed. I inhaled the odour of lemons. Behind her stood Hacker, in faded jeans and a loose shirt, his hair combed and a shy grin on his face. He was holding a shopping bag.

"Ted has something to say to you, Philip," said Corky Hacker, stepping inside. Hacker looked down at the floor and, advancing, stuck out a hand. "I'm sorry, Phil," he mumbled. "I was really being a jerk earlier today and I hereby apologize."

"Quite all right," I said, taking his hand and receiving a brief powerful squeeze.

Corky Hacker smiled triumphantly. "There now!

Don't you both feel better?" She lightly pushed the both of us. "You guys!" she said.

"Hullo you two," said Joan, opening the bathroom door. "Coming in for a drink then?"

"Thanks, Joanie," said Hacker, brightening. He held up the shopping bag.

"How about a game of Ruthless Landlord folks?"

Twelve

I abhor board games. When I was a child, I tried to conceal my disappointment on Christmas mornings as I unwrapped the games of Parcheesi and Snakes and Ladders that arrived from distant cousins. Above me in their chairs, my aunts smiled, but I sensed they shared my feelings about these silly pastimes. Among the bleakest memories of my childhood are those evenings in January when I sat in the library at The Gannymede, composing letters of gratitude to cousins in Boston and Vancouver, boys and girls whom I had never seen nor was ever likely to, but with whom the exchange of gifts and the subsequent epistolary falsehoods were decreed by family custom.

Joan, too, had never expressed much interest in throwing dice and moving pieces around a board. Actually she feels far too superior to be competitive. So, when Hacker withdrew the board from his shopping bag, I expected my wife to join me in declining his invitation. She was, however, busy making drinks and said nothing. Hacker dropped the game board on the bed.

"Have you folks ever played Ruthless Landlord? It's just the ticket for a rainy afternoon." He began to sing "What Do They Do on a Rainy Day in Rio?" He knew all the words and in fact was not a bad baritone. When he finished, the women laughed and from a balcony nearby there was applause. Hacker, who had obviously recovered his good humour, hurried to our open balcony door and cried, "Thank you, thank you, one and all!" Turning to us he said, "I'm sure when you were kids, you folks played all sorts of games."

"You'd be surprised," said Joan, handing him a drink.

"And you too, Phil, I bet."

"Well, of course," I said. Joan gave me a large whiskey and soda. "Every childhood has games of one sort or another and mine was no exception. As a matter of fact, my aunts were very particular about participation in play. I remember with fondness games of charades and Hide-and-Go-Seek. Up Jenkins of course."

"Oh," interrupted Hacker, "not those kind of games, Phil." Corky Hacker giggled.

"What sort were you thinking of?" I asked.

Hacker put his arm around my shoulders. "Did you never play any games out in the garage with the little girls down the street? You know what I mean? Sitting on the dusty seat from the old family Chev. Did you never spin the bottle, old son?"

"Spin the bottle? I can't say that I have. I remember Snap of course. And Old Maid."

Hacker guffawed. I hesitate to use that verb for it has always struck me as silly. But you must take my word for it; Hacker was the sort of man who guffawed.

"Ruthless Landlord is a hoot, Phil. You'll love it."

"It's a riot," said Corky Hacker.

"A riot," I repeated without much enthusiasm.

"And how does one play it?" asked Joan. She turned to me. "Another cocktail, Philip?"

"Yes, please."

"Well," said Hacker, sitting down on the bed. "It's really a variation of strip poker, only you play with a board and dice."

"It's a lot more fun than Passout," said Corky.

"It sounds jolly fun to me," Joan said. "My heavenly stars, I haven't played strip poker in years. Do let's have a go!"

"Good girl," said Hacker, grinning. "Are you game, Phil?"

"I'm afraid I'm not much for board games," I said. "But you three go ahead. Perhaps I'll go down to the bar with a book."

"Reading, reading, reading," said Joan sourly. "That's my Philip."

"Well, it's up to you, pal," Hacker said. "It's better with four, but I can play with the girls."

"If you do," said my wife, "you'll never get out alive."

"Oh, Philip," Corky said. "It's just a game. It's terrific fun."

"Well, only sometimes," said Hacker gravely. "It can, of course, get out of hand. I'm thinking of the Salisburys, Corky."

"Oh, Fred and Lorna, sure."

Hacker got up and walked around the room holding his hands behind his back as though he was delivering a lecture. "To tell you the truth, I never cared for Fred Salisbury. Just because he was a professor at the university did not entitle Fred to think he was that much swifter than the rest of us. In fact, in many ways Fred was a considerable dolt. Personally I think he was a Communist, too. His wife, however, was very nice. Of course, they were having problems."

"Oh yes," said Corky. "They had their problems, all right. I don't think they should have played that night."

"What happened?" I asked.

"Well, Fred kept losing," Corky said. "And it became very embarrassing. I really felt sorry for the man. And then Lorna kept making fun of him."

"True enough," said Hacker, "but Fred was not a good cork sport. I mean, sport, Cork. You have to admit that."

"That's true, Teddy."

"Anyway," Hacker continued, "he got down to his briefs."

"Then," said Corky, "he landed on his wife's property, poor guy. The Tippet and Wimple, wasn't it, Ted?"

"I believe, and my memory is better than fair about such matters, it was the Yashmak Eastern Café, Cork."

"And Fred wouldn't go for it."

"He wouldn't go to the buff," said Hacker, rocking on his heels. "That was it in the famous nutshell. We all agreed at the beginning and then Fred reneged. A very poor display, I thought."

"So," Corky said, "Lorna got on him."

"And rightly so," said Hacker. "Fred couldn't cut the mustard. A deal's a deal. The United States of America, the greatest country in the world, was built on agreements between people."

With the telling of this tale, Corky Hacker's eyes had widened with excitement. "So Lorna began to make these insinuating suggestions, saying maybe Fred was afraid. That he was maybe . . . well, you know . . ."

"*Inadequate* is the word you're casting about for, Corky," said her husband. "That's what the woman was suggesting."

"Anyway, it got really wild. They began to shout at one another and all kinds of stuff came out. The rest of us just sat there listening to all this."

"They opened a very large can of worms, all right," said Hacker, stroking his jaw. "It turned ugly, there's no question about it. Of course, they both had far too much to drink."

"But it doesn't have to be that way," Corky said.

"By no means," said Hacker. "It can be just a fun event among friends."

I swallowed half a glass of whiskey and club soda. "Why don't we play the Monkey Trick?" I asked. I was by now feeling a bit spunky and mischievous.

Hacker only shook his head slowly. "Oh, Corky and I have already had a game of that, Phil. You can't play the old Monkey Trick more than once in an afternoon. At least, I can't. And I would venture to suggest that it would take a pretty good man to play more than one game. Am I right in that regard, Cork?"

"You are right, Teddy," said his wife, nuzzling her face into his neck. "And you are a good man. You're the best." They embraced. It is always disconcerting to witness displays of marital affection, the more so in the light of the suspicion that many of them are contrived for the sake of appearance.

"Well," I said, "this Wretched Landowner, or whatever you call it, does not sound like my cup of tea."

"Suit yourself, pal," said Hacker. He and Corky were

now sitting on the floor. "Ruthless Landlord is certainly not for everyone."

"Ted," my wife said, "what you must understand is that Philip is very modest about such things." She was leaning against the dresser behind them.

"Is that a fact?" said Hacker. "Well, don't worry about it, Phil. It isn't everything. The way I look at it, old Mother Nature provides compensation. Some people can run fast while others are good at chess. Some people have big muscles but have to wear eyeglasses or perhaps a hearing appliance. Me, I have a bum ticker."

"And just what, may I ask, are you suggesting?"

"Me, Phil? I'm not suggesting anything."

He drained the contents of his glass and placed the vessel on top of his head. "May I have anower dwinkie, pwease?" he asked in a tiny voice. To my horror, Joan took the glass and said, "Ooo certainly may." I finished my drink feeling vaguely insulted.

"Well," I said, "it wouldn't be fair to play the game this way. I would have to get dressed."

"That, sir, only makes sense," said Hacker. "You and Joanie would, of course, have to put on more clothes. I mean, fair is fair, Phil."

Corky Hacker smiled at me and, reaching over, pressed my hand. "It's really fun, Philip."

Hacker observed us with amused eyes. "But we don't want any Salisbury shenanigans, Phil. No tantrums if you are beset by Dame Fortune. Play hard, but play fair." He took the drink from Joan without a word and, leaning forward, abruptly shouted,

Huskers up and Huskers down
Huskers all around the town.
Go you Huskers, go, go, go!

From the unseen balcony came more scattered applause. The whiskey buzzed in my startled ears as I listen to my own voice softly chant,

Gannymede, Gannymede
Gannymede Man!
If anyone can do it,
The Gannymede can.
Gooooooo you Gannies.

For a moment Hacker and I stared at one another with hatred. Then he took another huge drink and grinned. "Way to go, fellah! Way to be! Let the game commence."

I had been sitting on the bed and when I stood up I realized that I was mildly drunk. Standing at the small wardrobe by the bed I selected my clothes with care and, holding a fresh drink, retired to the bathroom to dress.

Inside that small tiled room I briefly regretted my decision to participate in Hacker's nonsense. I felt I had somehow been trapped by a devious intelligence into something that could only end in disaster. In this melodramatic humour I laid out my clothes. I could hear the murmur of their voices and their laughter. I imagined they were talking about me and I once pressed my ear against the door but could hear nothing intelligible. As I pulled on a pair of long dark hose and fastened my garters, I was possessed by the underdog's fanatical sense of grievance. Let them connive, I thought as I climbed into my boxer shorts. For the first time in my life I stared into the victim's heart, remembering how Merton Uttley, a rich, stupid boy with no discernibly redeeming qualities, had nearly drowned in Bald Pond years ago during the school's cross-country run. How Merton had run his heart out in the November Classic, and how he must have felt as he was pulled exhausted from the freezing water hours after the others had crossed the line!

Inspired, I put on an undershirt, a short-sleeved white shirt and school tie, white duck pants, blue blazer, and brogans. I then placed a white yachting cap upon my head. This was my Bermuda Cricket Tour Costume; it was especially appropriate for a drink at the club after the match. I had brought these clothes to Mexico against the chance that we might meet some interesting people for cocktails. Checking myself in the mirror I was heartened by the notion that it would take a very great deal of losing for me to emerge unclothed. I was also encouraged by the realization that I might very well be vouchsafed a view of splendid Corky Hacker *in puris naturalibus*. I left the bathroom feeling gay (if I may use that word as it was once intended to be used).

Joan immediately raised a glass. "Here he is, ladies and gentlemen! Clifton Webb himself." Her reference to the late Mr. Webb did not bother me. What did, however, in a mild way, was the fact that Joan was now fully dressed. Either she had put on her clothes before the eyes of our guests, or they had somehow averted their gaze; in either case it suggested a degree of intimacy one should not expect from persons who had been complete strangers only the day before. Joan leaned against the dresser in a pair of slacks which snugly fit her large round bottom. There was also a denim shirt which she had cunningly knotted above the naval to display several inches of bare midriff. Her thick, dark blonde hair had been pulled back into a ponytail and she had painted her lips. The effect was provocative.

Corky Hacker, still on the floor beside her husband, looked up at me. "Wow, do you ever look elegant, Philip!"

I bowed stiffly. "Thank you, my dear."

Hacker wagged his head. "You're the berries all right, Phil. Where would you wear an outfit like that anyway?"

I laughed. "Well, Ted, as the man said, 'If you have to ask . . .'"

I brandished my empty glass. "On with the game! And another cocktail, if you please."

Corky Hacker covered her mouth and Joan smiled. Hacker watched me closely. "I'll bet he wears that kind of thing to his school's annual costume party. Right, Joanie?"

"Wrong, Ted," said Joan.

"Where shall we play?" I asked. "They don't seem to have provided us with an activity table."

"How about on the floor?" asked Corky Hacker. "That's where we played the other time. At the Salisburys'."

"On the floor?" I asked, with mock outrage in my voice.

"Sure," said Hacker. "Why the hell not? You too good

to sit on the floor with the rest of us? Afraid to get your nice white pants dirty?"

"Ted, please," said Corky.

"Not at all, my dear," I said. "I shall descend for the nonce. It is, after all, only a game."

"Damn right," said Hacker, emptying the contents of his glass down his throat and handing the glass to Joan. "Get me another drink."

Joan took the glass. "And what's the magic word, Ted?" she asked.

'Oh, guess I please. I mean please, I guess," said Hacker glumly. "Let's set up the board."

He looked so peevish that, acting on a basic principle of gamesmanship, I began to rub my hands together, simulating enthusiastic optimism.

Hacker's disposition improved, however, when, with the initial toss of the dice, he won the role of banker. In any game, the banker, if he is clever and dishonest, enjoys an advantage over other players since he can pilfer funds. I decided that Hacker would bear watching. For those of you unfamiliar with the game of Ruthless Landlord, I can only say that, like most board games, it is predicated on vicious sadism and an aptitude for inflicting humiliation on your opponents.

After throwing the dice, a contestant moves his "piece" (miniature parts of the human anatomy, viz: a tiny phallus, a pair of breasts, a lady's leg, etc.) around a board upon which are listed various properties, streets and shops and so on, each site denoting an item of apparel. And so you have places like Petticoat Lane, The Blue Tabard Inn, Knickerbocker Alley, La Peignoir, and the Balmoral House. When the player lands upon a property that is unsold, he may, if he wishes, buy it from the bank for the listed price. After all the properties have been sold, the game begins in earnest, for then rents can be charged.

Hacker explained that in Ruthless Landlord the rent is extracted in the form of clothing, and that what you are obliged to remove must correspond roughly with the name on the particular property. So, if you land, for example on Ulster Street, you are expected to remove your Ulster, and if you don't happen to be wearing one, the next best thing, your Burberry, say. A preternaturally silly game as you can imagine!

We all began to play with enthusiasm. Hacker enjoyed a remarkable run of luck and took great pleasure in chiding me on my perverse misfortune. "Tough mutton, Phil," he would say as I read aloud the "Rag Bag" card instructing me to go to the nearest tailor for repairs. Both women also had good fortune, and there was brisk trading among all three of my opponents. Within an hour they had completed deals which left Hacker owning most of one side of the board, while Joan controlled the other, and Corky Hacker the adjacent properties. This was indeed a formidable gauntlet. My acquisitions, meanwhile, were scattered and of little value, comprising a mall named after a famous English general who wore high boots, a bistro called the Panama Club, and the seldom-visited Farthingale Theatre.

I began to lose badly, feeling much as the small homeowner must in the face of relentless corporate development. In a damnable streak of bad luck, I landed on Cardigan Row (Hacker's), The Bib & Tucker Restaurant (Hacker's), The Cocked Hat (Joan's), The Pump Room

(Joan's), and Gaskins' Boutique (Corky Hacker's). That tour cost me my jacket, shirt and school tie, yachting cap, brogans, and hosiery with garters, the latter occasioning considerable mirth in the Hackers, who confessed to never having seen such accoutrements.

Hacker was elated. "By golly, this calls for another snort," he said, getting to his feet. After discovering that we had finished the whiskey, he was soon telephoning room service. On his next roll he landed alongside me on his wife's Island of Jersey and, cheerfully peeling off his shirt, displayed a large hairless chest. This he promptly began to beat with both fists. At the same time he startled us all with an imitation of Tarzan beckoning his assorted jungle friends. A moment later we heard Fred Flintstone reply in kind from a nearby balcony. Hacker chuckled. "Lordy, this has just got to be the greatest holiday I've ever had."

Joan lost her sandals and displayed her long gruesome-looking feet. "Aren't my feet beautiful?" she asked.

"No, they're not," said Corky Hacker, and everyone laughed, including Joan.

When the knock came on the door, I had removed everything except my underpants. Amid my castoffs, I sat on the floor, a pale fakir enduring the taunts that were thrown my way. "Philip," said Corky, "has the most adorable little pot-belly."

"A fine figure of a man," said Hacker. "A little light in the hams, perhaps." He still wore his pants. Joan was now wearing only a brassiere and bikini panties, though this was scarcely more breathtaking than the three handkerchiefs worn by most of the women around the swimming pool that morning. The beautiful Corky, however, had us completely fooled. Beneath the terry-cloth jacket she wore the striped fisherman's jersey and a pair of respectable white shorts. She was in fact dressed for the dining room. Yet the four of us in our various states of undress, and seated on the floor, must have presented a singular eyeful to the little brown man who entered the room carrying aloft a tray of cold beer. He did not look particularly disapproving, though I am told the local Indians are a chaste people. This may account for the man's willingness to testify at my trial next month on the subject of loose sexual practices among *los norteamericanos*.

As the afternoon wore away, I began to lose a feeling of fellowship and, like a solitary tavern drinker who feels isolated from the revellers around him, began to harbour a grievance. Please bear in mind that I had been consuming alcohol since the noon hour and was by then rather fuddled with drink. Is it any wonder that many details of the late afternoon are not forthcoming and probably never will be? I was, however, sure with the steadfast certainty of the aggrieved or the mad that Hacker was cheating. More than once I thought he counted his piece incorrectly and thus avoided landing on someone's property. But I couldn't catch him. I myself was having difficulty counting, and surreptitiously resorted to my fingers when the numbers on the dice exceeded four. Still I watched him closely, determined, as only an obsessive maniac can be, with finding him out. Because of this concentration I fell silent, and several times Joan admonished me about sulking. "Don't be a poor loser, darling," she said. "Have some more beer."

"What big teeth you have!" I answered.

"The better to bite off your little button, my adorable one."

"Drink up, Phil," said Hacker, pouring some beer into my glass. "We're on vacation."

"So we are, Ted, so we are!" I smiled grimly at them all but kept my counsel. From somewhere (a balcony radio?) came the insane music of a mariachi band and Hacker hummed along with the tune. When I looked up from the board, a curtain of darkness had abruptly descended over sea and sky. In a word it was night. Someone switched on a lamp.

It was then that I caught Hacker cheating. I remember he rolled eight, and that should have put him on my Farthingale Theatre. Instead, Hacker moved his piece only as far as the preceding square which, as it turned out, was the innocuous Free Fitting. "Now, just a minute," I said, trying to conceal the outrage in my voice. "You just rolled eight. That puts you in attendance at Farthingale Theatre, which, in case it has escaped your attention, happens to be part of my holdings, slender though they may be."

Hacker smiled. "How do you figure that, Phil? As you say, I rolled eight. That fact is indisputable, and the dice are there for everyone to see. Thusly and so, if you go back to Cordwainer Crescent where I was, and count eight spots ahead, you cannot help but land on Free Fitting." He reached for a Free Fitting card, and I surprised myself by smacking the back of his hand.

Corky Hacker, who had been dozing, opened her eyes, and Joan said, "Philip! Really!"

"You're not getting away with it again, Hacker," I cried. My voice, I'm afraid, was rising. "Your piece was on that funeral home, The Shroud. Not Cordwainer Crescent."

"Now, Phil," said Hacker gently, "is this necessary? We're just whiling away a rainy day with a friendly game."

"Except that you're winning all the time!"

"Oh, Philip," said Joan. "Don't be absurd!"

"Shut up! I wouldn't be at all surprised if you're in on this, too. There's something damn fishy going on here."

"Look, my friend," said Hacker, "I was definitely on Cordwainer Crescent. Was I not, ladies?"

"I think so, Ted, yes," said Joan.

With a dreamy smile Corky settled her head against Hacker's shoulder. "I'm sorry, but I wasn't looking. Let's go to bed, Teddy Bear!"

"You were at the funeral home, Hacker," I said, moving his piece to the Farthingale Theatre.

"My dear Phil," he said, returning his pair of diminutive buttocks to Free Fitting, "these cavils must cease. You're certainly not being a very good sport about all this. I can understand as well as the next man, the frustration in defeat . . ."

"Ted's right, Philip," said Joan. "You're behaving like a child."

"I am *not* behaving like a child," I said, pointing at Hacker. "It is he who is not playing the game. He's been cheating all along. He's been cheating all of us."

Hacker shook his head. "Shades of Fred Salisbury," he murmured. "Remember, hon?"

Corky Hacker yawned and nodded. "Uh-huh."

"Never mind Fred Salisbury," I demanded. "You landed on my property, so take off something, Hacker. Your pants will do."

"Philip!" said Joan. "Do please be a dear and stop shouting. You're making quite an ass of yourself."

"Be a nice Philip," said Corky. With her eyes closed she snuggled against her husband.

"Your husband has been cheating," I said. "As far as I'm concerned that renders the contest null and void."

"A gross calumny," said Hacker, measuring out a glass of beer.

"I appeal to everyone's sense of fair play."

"No one saw him but you, my darling," said Joan.

"That's just what he wants," I shouted. "He's been distracting us all along while he moves his piece to safe territory."

Hacker addressed his glass of beer.

If you can keep your head
When all about you
Are losing theirs and blaming it on you
If you can trust yourself when all men doubt you
But make allowances for their doubting too.

I now stood over the three of them in some state, I suppose, of alcoholic derangement. "A man," I declared, "who cheats at simple board games is lower than a worm."

Like his wife, Hacker had now closed his eyes. The two of them swayed beneath me as Hacker recited.

Teach us delight in simple things
And mirth that has no bitter springs
Forgiveness free of evil done
And love to all men 'neath the sun!

This was greeted by a tremendous burst of applause from our unseen audience. There followed more mariachi music and the hectic tempo of the cornets and guitars flayed my shredded nerves. By the moment I grew angrier and more confused, warning all within a hundred yards that Hacker was a seducer and a mountebank. After this disgraceful exhibition there were cries from the balconies of "Shame, shame" and "Sit down, man, for goodness sakes." (How did they know I was standing? I wonder.)

The music increased in volume and the telephone rang. I felt my legs trembling and, past all shame, I staggered to the bed. Hacker was soon speaking into the telephone and I lay there, a drunken schoolmaster on holiday, listening to him. "Don't worry your head about it, Captain," he said. "We're lowering the pressure immediately. I have my eye on the gauge at this very moment. The patient is now under sedation and, to coin a phrase which you probably have in your own tongue, our lips are sealed."

The women meantime attended to me; Corky Hacker covered me with a blanket while Joan rubbed my feet, which had grown unaccountably cold. "My poor darling," she said. "You must rest now."

Corky Hacker placed a warm hand against my cheek and I may have kissed that hand. It smelled of ice cream and lemon Cokes and the presence of that Nebraska housewife in her fisherman's jersey and white shorts awakened the memory of a summer day I may have lived through or only dreamed about. I heard Hacker say, "I'll hang up his nice white pants."

Joan mentioned something about going out for dinner, but I was asleep before the others replied.

Thirteen

Apparently they are not going to hang me or shoot me. "We are not barbarians, Señor Bannister," said Mr. Gomez with a note of disapproval in his voice. At the behest of Thrust and Parry, Mr. Gomez flies down once a week from Mexico City to consult with the people involved in my case. After he has finished his business with the authorities, he looks in on me. But he is clearly not happy with the circumstances. Last week he confessed to me that he finds criminal law rather squalid. He has spent most of his life in estate management and has done very well for himself; he now has several young lawyers working for him in his Mexico City offices. Mr. Gomez, a short, plump, elderly man in a lightweight suit and a nifty straw fedora, never stays for long; he finds it uncomfortable talking to criminals. And, although he is too polite to say so, I know he thinks I have besmirched the good name of The Gannymede with these scandalous murders.

Mr. Gomez is an old Gannymedian. He was one of the first citizens of Mexico to attend the school and both his son and his grandson have followed in his footsteps, as the saying goes. His grandson is currently enrolled in grade six, a fact I did not know, but then I had little to do with the Junior School. Mr. Gomez showed me a picture of a little Gomez, plump and brown like his grandpa; he was wearing shorts and soccer jersey and standing in front of the chapel. This photograph of my old school moved me, and Mr. Gomez, nodding with sympathy, gave me time to comport myself. All the same, both of us would rather talk about the school than about my crimes, and so we gossip about old days at The Gannymede and particularly about hockey. When Mr. Gomez was at the school back in the thirties, he developed a passion for hockey. He still follows the fortunes of the varsity team by reading the winter issue of *The Gannymedian*.

When our conversation reluctantly turns to my impending trial for murder, Mr. Gomez sighs and sips at the orange juice laid out by Miguel, who is very impressed by my *abrogado* from Mexico City. Mr. Gomez then glances into his shiny black attaché case at the few miserable papers there. "This is all such a bad business, Señor Bannister," he says, consulting the thin gold watch on his wrist. "Well, I'm afraid I must be off or I will miss my plane. "Say, have you read the latest *Gannymedian*? But perhaps the alumni office does not have your current address. I will get on to Buddy Keeler about that. The team is having an exceptional year, by the way. They have beaten Bollocks Hall twice. That young Hotchkiss is a remarkable player. I was at school with his grandfather, you know. He, too, was a fine athlete, but an unpleasant lad and I'm afraid a bigot. He gave me a very difficult time of it. I remember once at evening prayers. We had evening prayers in those days." Mr. Gomez shrugs at the memory. "Ah, it's water over the bridge now. But say, this grandson of his! He can certainly put the old biscuit in the cage. Five goals against Opposite Academy!"

Mr. Gomez shakes his head. "I would give anything to see him play in the new arena." He smiles at me. "Remember the old unheated arena, Señor Bannister? The cold was something, was it not? A February afternoon and everybody's breath going up like smoke. I remember it so well. We all dressed in mufflers and scarves with woollen hats on our heads and mittens on our hands. We carried our little wooden rattles. Remember those? You rotated them at the end of a stick and they made a racket for you. And the cheers!"

We've got the T . . . E . . . A . . . M
That's on the B . . . E . . . A . . . M
We've got the team
That's on the beam
That's really hep to the jive.
Come on, Gannies, skin 'em alive!

Mr. Gomez slaps his fat little knees and stands up. "Now I really must be off or I will never catch that plane. I will see you next week, señor. They are treating you all right in here? No monkey business, I trust? If they beat you, give me particulars. I will probably need to make some kind of report." Now that he is leaving, Mr. Gomez is in a much better mood and he favours me with a smile. "Do not become discouraged, Señor Bannister. You are going through a tough time, there is no doubt about that. But an old Gannymedian never says die. Is that not so?"

"It is so, Señor Gomez."

"Exactly," he says picking up my tin dinner plate and banging it against the bars of my cell. "Jailer!" he shouts. Mr. Gomez is too polite to speak Spanish in my presence.

Upon hearing this command, Miguel shuffles into view wearing a pair of bedroom slippers that once belonged to his former employer, the late Miss Dodge.

"Open, dog," orders Mr. Gomez, and the old man bends to his task, carefully averting his bad eye from my visitor. As Miguel has told me, it doesn't do to offend a man of Mr. Gomez's dignity by reminding him that disfigurement and ugliness also inhabit the world. One would never earn a rich man's coin that way, says my shrewd old custodian.

After Mr. Gomez leaves, Miguel brews some coffee for both of us and sometimes I will pick up one of Miss Dodge's books and read a passage to the old man. He is already in love with England. His favourite book is *Harold, the Last of the Saxon Kings* by Sir Edward Bulwer-Lytton. Time and time again he asks me to read the famous opening lines, which admittedly are enticing.

> *Merry was the month of May in the year of our Lord 1052. Few were the boys and few the lasses, who overslept themselves on the first of that buxom month. Long ere the dawn, the young crowds had sought mead and woodland, to cut poles and wreathe flowers.*

Fourteen

The ruins of the city of Tulum attract thousands of tourists each year. You can take the morning ferry from Cozumel across the straits of Quintana Roo to Playa del Carmen. The ferry ride takes less than two hours. At Playa del Carmen you board a bus and travel for another hour through the jungle until you arrive at a crossroads in the middle of Nowhere. From Nowhere you follow other tourists as they straggle down a side road toward the old walled city which was built on a great cliff overlooking the Caribbean. I myself found the ruins undistinguished. The entire place with its stalls of trinkets and blankets, its little cabanas and souvenir booths, looked very tatty to me. However, I chiefly remember Tulum because it was there that Ted Hacker tried to push me off the cliffs into the sea.

The morning after the infamous game, I awakened, not surprisingly, with both an atrocious headache and an oppressive sense of guilt over my conduct of the previous evening. I was unclear as to exactly what I said, but I had the drunkard's uneasy suspicion that I had made vile and unforgivable utterances.

That Hacker was an oaf seemed beyond dispute. Yet had he done me harm enough to provoke such vituperation? Moreover, were the women not partly right in claiming for him an extravagant geniality that I was unable to appreciate? As I lay thinking about these matters, one fact seemed clear enough—I had not behaved like a gentleman.

It was just after seven o'clock and the hotel was quiet. From where I lay, I could see a bit of fresh blue sky. In the next bed, Joan, wearing her Lone Ranger mask, snored faintly. She always put on the sleeping patches after a late night; the next day they performed the function of a Do Not Disturb sign. Accordingly, I performed my morning toilet as quietly as possible and slipped from the room.

In the lobby the pallid clerk was asleep over his newspaper and did not stir as I walked past. The dining room was not yet open for breakfast, and so I decided to walk into the village. It was a wise decision. The clear morning air eased my headache and the freshness of the day was inspiring. Birds squawked and gabbled in the wet trees as the sunlight burned off the mist from the jungle. On the other side of the road the Caribbean sparkled. Within a half hour I was seated at a sidewalk restaurant enjoying a meal of eggs and toast and coffee. The town was still quiet and the restaurant only half-filled. A waiter sprinkled water over the wooden floor and swept it clean. At a corner table by a cageful of parrots sat Mr. Yoshimodo, looking very smart in a tropical suit the colour of oatmeal. He was busy at his breakfast.

I was on my second cup of coffee when a taxi braked sharply across the street and I saw Ted Hacker leaning out the rear window. He was wearing his mirror sunglasses and pointing at me. "There he is!" Hacker cried. All three soon piled out of the car. Hacker, in jeans and loose-fitting shirt, was wearing a hard straw hat. His wife, bare-legged in a denim skirt and dark blouse, took his hand as they waited for traffic to pass. Joan, in bright yellow slacks and a green blouse, had large sunglasses on her face. They hurried across the street toward me and I braced myself for a lecture on intemperance. "What do you say, podner?" asked Hacker. "How's the old bean this morning?" Corky Hacker clung to his arm and smiled at me as Joan bent over and kissed my cheek. "My darling. You don't look at all well. Your colour is poor."

"I feel fine, all things considered. I took some aspirin a while ago. The walk into town helped, too."

"What you need, Phil, is a bit of fresh sea air," said Hacker. "That will bring the rosies and the posies back to your cheeks." At a nearby table a middle-aged man looked up from his paperback and inspected Hacker over the rim of his reading glasses.

"Finish your coffee, darling," Joan said. "We're off to Tulum and the ferry leaves in ten minutes."

"It's a famous historic site," Hacker said. "Supposed to be worth seeing." The man with the paperback continued to gawk at Hacker.

I suppose I might have resisted; I resented all these plans made in my absence. Yet I also felt that I ought perhaps to atone for my sins of the previous evening. By now people were hurrying along the jetty to the boat: tourists with cameras and large hats, and Indian families carrying bundles fastened by string. Vendors hawked oranges and ice cream from their bicycle wagons and in the sunlight people looked happy. I paid my bill and we walked to the ticket booth.

Leaning against the rail on the crowded upper deck of the little ferry I felt happy. I understand that travelling on water often affects people this way. The hot, oily smell of marine engines and the cries of seabirds overhead and the noisy restless passengers left me wishing I had spent more time at sea. It was thirty years since I had travelled on water and that was by canoe at summer camp on Big Toe Lake. Now Captain Bannister, listening to the satisfying creak of the fittings, joined others in waving farewell to strangers as the ferry's horn hooted and we left the pier. Beside me Hacker busily snapped pictures of the retreating island with its white hotels and beaches and palm trees. He had given the straw hat to his wife so that when he leaned over the railing with his camera, his blond hair blew wildly in the wind. This made him look somehow innocent and vulnerable, and it made me feel even more guilty for having so abused him. He was, after all, just another tourist stealing a few leisurely days from the treadmill. Selling pills to grumpy doctors in Minnesota on winter mornings could not be much fun. And here he was like a large happy child with his camera and the splendid day before him.

He stopped with his photography and breathed deeply. "Isn't this great, Phil! Smell that air. I'll bet there's no pollution in that." He laughed. "Just think of all those poor guys back home shovelling their driveways! This has got to be the best holiday I've ever had. I'm sure glad we met you and Joanie."

I gazed across the water and said, "I'm sorry, Hacker." I turned to him. He was frowning at me. "All right, Ted," I said. He smiled and looked away. "I mean," I said, "about last night."

Hacker began to fiddle with his camera but then stopped and again looked at me. He pushed the sunglasses back on his hair and squinted at me in the sunlight. Around us other tourists gestured at the sea and shouted over the heavy throb of the engines. Only the Indian families sat along the benches, watchful and silent.

"I said I'm sorry about last night," I repeated loudly.

Hacker looked away again. He seemed thoughtful. "Don't worry about it. You had a snootful. It was really my fault. I should have realized that you weren't used to that kind of thing."

I was impressed by his reasonable tone. "But I should not have drunk so much or carried on the way I did. It was a lack of character on my part."

"Not really, Phil. It was my fault entirely." He continued to stare at the horizon. "And that goofy game! Boy, was that a mistake! I mean, some people are embarrassed by things like that. I should have known that someone like you . . ." He looked solemn. Were the tears in his eyes caused by the wind? "I stepped out of line, Phil, and I'm sorry. Can we shake on it?"

"It's not really necessary, Ted."

"Maybe not, but I'd appreciate it."

Out of the corner of my eye I could see Mr. Yoshimodo in his porridge-coloured suit. From behind his sunglasses Mr. Yoshimodo watched Hacker and me shake hands like old friends.

"I feel a lot better now," said Hacker, looking out to sea again. After several moments of silence he said, "Look, Phil. If Joanie says anything about last night, just forget it. Okay?"

"Well, I can't see that she did anything wrong. After all, it was I . . ."

Hacker shook his head. "No no no no. I'm not talking

about that. I'm talking about what happened after you . . ." He cleared his throat. "After you passed out." He looked at me. "I hope you won't take it the wrong way. These things happen on holidays. Perhaps the three of us got carried away, but when people are far from home, can you really blame them? Is it not reasonable to leave your cares behind and have a little fun, for heaven's sake? You just have to talk to people who work in resorts. They'll tell you some hair-raising tales."

"And just what are you referring to, Ted?" I asked. "Just what exactly did go on?" I hesitated, nearly choking on the dreadful phrase. "After I passed out?"

Hacker looked away. "Please remember the extenuating circumstances, Phil. Keep them in mind. We all had a very great deal to drink." He laughed. "Nearly too much in my case but not quite."

"Now listen," I said, moving closer. I had the feeling our conversation had grown interesting to others. "Listen." My mouth was inches from Hacker's large ear. "You'd better tell me what went on last night, damn it."

Hacker stepped back, unsmiling. "Well, you don't have to get huffy, Phil. You don't have to bite my head off. You yourself behaved badly. You've just admitted as much. You apologized for your swinish behaviour and rightly so. And I accepted the apology. Joanie and Cork and I forgive you. Now all I'm doing is asking the same of you. A little forgiveness and understanding go a long way in this dreary old world, Phil."

I looked up at the clear sky and the bright, quivering air over the ship's smokestack. I saw Hacker suspended headfirst over that large heated funnel, while I held his ankles and counted to three.

"Am I to understand?" I asked. "That you and your wife and Joan . . ."

Hacker placed his hand on my shoulder. "Listen, Phil, go easy on Joanie. All right? She's a wonderful human being. I've probably said this before but it bears repeating, you're a very lucky man." He grinned and handed me the camera. "Now, how about taking my picture? Ham that I am, I can't resist a snap. For my dear old mom and dad at home. Please."

He leaned against the rail and I took his picture. A few moments later our wives joined us and Hacker insisted on taking more photographs. Then Mr. Yoshimodo approached and asked shyly if we would like a picture of the four of us. "Why, thanks, my friend," said Hacker, applying the flat of his hand to the robot salesman's shoulder blades. Mr. Yoshimodo took several pictures of us linked arm in arm on the deck of the ferry. I understand these photographs are now in the hands of the authorities.

A half hour later we sighted the mainland, a low line of sand and trees. A half hour beyond that we had landed at Playa del Carmen, a pokey-looking settlement with a few stucco hotels and a long beach. There we boarded a bus that had doubtless seen duty on highways in Pennsylvania or California thirty years ago. I know nothing of transmissions or gearboxes, but regard it as unusual when a driver uses his right foot to kick the gear lever into place. Blue smoke seeped through the floorboards but was soon carried away by the rushing air from the open windows. The driver, who seemed to be in a savage temper, drove very fast. None of the passengers, Indian or otherwise, said much; instead, we all gaped out at the scrubby jungle hurtling past the windows. At the front of the bus a radio blared crazy Mexican rock-and-roll. And so, in this rocket-shaped relic from the fifties, we sped sixty miles into the country to Nowhere.

At Nowhere (a gas station and two cafés) we stepped down from the bus into vivid noon sunlight and, like pilgrims, followed a score of other tourists down a side road through the bush. I was a long way from my beloved school with its fine old buildings and playing fields. Ahead of us hiked Mr. Yoshimodo, followed by a young family. The tall, pale husband in farmer's overalls had a spade beard. His wife wore a long skirt and shawl and there was a baby riding in a carrier on her back. Behind them walked a man who looked like Fred Flintstone's brother. Hacker fanned his brow with the straw hat. "Good gravy, it's a scorcher," he said, walking alongside Joan, who had tied a kerchief to her head. In the tight yellow pants her backside looked bigger than the day before. Or was that only my imagination? I wondered how many hands (and belonging to whom?) had clutched and grabbed at that flesh while I lay sleeping away my drunkenness. I hope that some of my former students who may even now be reading these words will heed the warning of their old English teacher: beware of the perils of drink; the good ladies of the Women's Christian Temperance Union have been right all along.

Corky Hacker and I soon fell behind the others. Without a word she took my hand, though she seemed as shy as a schoolgirl and now and then looked down at her tennis shoes. Finally she said, "You're awfully quiet today, Philip. What are you thinking about?"

"I'm wondering just what went on last night. Among the three of you, I mean. After I . . . went to sleep."

"Oh, that," she said, and looked away at a large dead tree that was white as bone. There were several of these arboreal skeletons in the landscape.

"Yes, that," I said.

She sighed. "It wasn't important."

"Oh, wasn't it?" I said, annoyed by her casual dismissal of infidelity. "Well, some people might think otherwise." I knew I sounded stuffy but couldn't help myself. I, after all, can be a stuffy person. "To think," I continued, "that three respectable middle-class citizens could, on very short notice indeed, participate in some kind of revolting ménage à trois."

Corky Hacker looked at me. "What's that?"

"It's simply French for a relationship among three people. It usually means one of the married partners has a lover and the three of them accept this arrangement."

"Oh," she said. "I thought it was a position."

"A position?"

"Yes. Like Soixante-neuf or the Venetian Concertina."

I glanced sideways at her rounded cheek, her fine skin and bright American eye, now downcast. "You know the Venetian Concertina?" She made a face I imagined her once making when Daddy inquired after the identity of the awful boy in the red convertible.

"Oh, Philip, let's not talk about it anymore. After all, there is more to life than physical relationships."

"Perhaps so, but I believe I'm entitled . . ."

"Philip," she said primly. "I don't wish to discuss it any further. The subject is *c . . . l . . . o . . . s . . . e . . . d.*"

We had now reached the outskirts of Tulum and were walking past shabby restaurants open to the road and thatched-roof sheds where one could buy hats and dresses and native trinkets worked in silver. Ahead lay the lichened grey stones of the old town.

Corky Hacker tightened her grip on my hand. "Oh look, Philip! Look at the funny old place! It must be really old."

Hacker and Joan stood waiting for us on a rise of pale worn grass where you could see the steps of the temple ascending to the sky.

"Maybe," said Hacker, "we should have a bite of lunch before we tackle those babies."

"A splendid idea," said Joan. "I'm famished."

At one of the restaurants we drank beer and ate some hideous bean concoction. Around us other tourists poked among the racks of long dresses or selected postcards. In the dusty street by a tour bus, that proverbial slacker, the Mexican mongrel, lay sleeping on his side. But even in the strong vertical sunlight the place looked dingy and mean. A stench of decay and ordure hung about this corner of the world, and I found myself longing for a crisp winter afternoon in the temperate zone. Hacker had bought a guidebook and to my annoyance read aloud from it during the meal. His wife sat next to me on the wooden bench and pressed her warm thigh against mine.

• • •

After lunch we explored the ruins, walking listlessly among the stone buildings and peering at the faded images behind the bars of the Temple de los Frescos. We had again wordlessly divided into two teams. Ahead of us Hacker took Joan's hand and helped her up the narrow steps of the Castillo while I climbed beside Corky. Near the top Mr. Yoshimodo was almost bent over as he felt his way skyward. He had fashioned a handkerchief into a kind of hat and this now covered his sleek dark hair. He looked oddly comical in his new suit and with this bean-picker's hat on his head.

Halfway up, Corky Hacker stopped and looked back at the green expanse of the Yucatán jungle. "Wow! This is something, isn't it, Phil! It's a long way down."

"We've a way to go yet," I said, looking at the film of moisture along her upper lip. Her shirt was stained at the armpits and she had opened the top buttons. I saw the swell of her breasts in a black brassiere and she caught me looking.

Smiling, she said, "You naughty boy."

We gazed at one another and then continued to clamber over the warm stones under that dreadful sun.

At the summit we stood holding hands, enjoying the breeze off the ocean which stretched eastward below us. Surf broke over the long magnificent beach and I was excited by Corky Hacker's presence. There in the violent sunlight I was stricken by lust while around us other sightseers looked into storerooms and chambers where the Maya had once worshipped or fornicated. We, too, moved along the narrow pathways until we reached a small stone cell. It might once have been the quarters of a holy man who went there to meditate or perform some hocus-pocus before officiating at some poor devil's sacrifice. Or was it the Aztec who threw people off cliffs? I'm afraid I'm not conversant with the barbaric rituals of Amerindian civilizations, though I suspect they were no more ruthless than those of my own ancestors in the forests of Europe. Visiting historic sites is nearly always ruinous to a hopeful view of mankind.

We stopped to enter the little stone room. It was cool and dark as a fruit cellar; the only light came from a small window that looked seaward. I suppose it had been cut into the wall to admit the rays of the rising sun. The Maya, or so I read in Hacker's guidebook, considered the rising sun powerful medicine. I stood by the tiny aperture looking down at the green water and trying to imagine some half-naked Indian standing where I now stood and waiting for the sunrise on some long-ago Monday morning. Around us were the voices of other tourists, and beside me Corky Hacker shivered. "It's cold in here, isn't it? You really notice it after the sunshine. Look at me! I've got goosebumps." She hugged her arms and shuddered.

Bannister the Gallant (and the Lustful) took her at once into his arms. It seemed natural for us to embrace and soon we were kissing passionately. Nearby a North American voice mentioned something about Balboa. "No no, Christ no," said her companion. "You're thinking about Cortéz. The Spaniards were here long before the Italians. Jesus, it's hot!"

Against that abrupt shaft of light by the little window overlooking the green sea I touched Corky Hacker's breast. She sighed and broke away from my grasp. "Oh dear," she said and caressed my face. "I'm sorry. I didn't mean for us to do that. I don't know what got into me." She took my hand and, kissing it, pressed it against her cheek like a tender lover. "Dearest Philip," she whispered.

The voices drew nearer and the man said, "I wonder what this little place was used for?" We could now hear their footsteps on the dry stones.

"We'd better go," said Corky.

"Where can we meet?" I asked.

She placed a finger on my lips. "We must be very, very careful, Philip." Clasping hands we made our way along the corridor where we met the historian and his wife, a couple in their middle years in matching blue outfits. They had to back out to allow us egress and we emerged blinking into the sunlight. Ted Hacker stood watching us. Corky ran and put her arms around him. "Hi hon," she said, clinging to him and looking up at him. "Isn't this something?" She removed his straw hat and put it on her own head. Hacker appeared to ignore her and watched only my approach.

"Hi," I said. "Where's Joan?"

He jerked his thumb over his shoulder. "Back there taking pictures," he said coldly.

Corky reached up and kissed the tip of her husband's nose. "That's my big bear." Like a statue Hacker paid her no mind. "I'm going to find Joanie," said Corky and hurried away. I watched her disappear among the tourists.

"Why don't you and I take a walk, Phil," said Hacker. His voice sounded dull and flat; the voice of the headmaster summoning a transgressor at the end of chapel to an ambulatory lecture on the vacancy of mind exhibited by boys who break wind during prayers. From my classroom window I used often to see Dr. Peach with hands clasped behind his back accompanying some lout down the avenue of oak trees at the front of the school.

Now Hacker walked moodily beside me as we stepped down to the rocks and grass behind the temple. Here a narrow path led to the edge of the great cliff. Over the years the wind from the sea had shaped and stunted the bushes around us, and below us the green waves broke and thundered onto the beach. "Phil," said Hacker, touching my elbow, "I am an extremely jealous man. I wish I weren't, but I am. This unfortunate trait may be inherited, or it may simply come from living with a beautiful woman and seeing others less fortunate than myself try to purloin a kiss or a feel at parties and other functions. In any event, I thought since you would have no way of knowing this, I ought to warn you." He stopped and, plucking off his glasses, smiled at me. "But let us not tarry on such a disagreeable theme! Why should there be rancour between us?" He stood with his hands on his hips and stared at the grey shadows of the temple's seawall. "It makes you think, doesn't it?" he said.

"What about?" I asked. I was annoyed by his presumptuous air of injury. The night before he had been intimate with my wife and now he was issuing warnings about my getting involved with his wife.

"Why, these ruins!" he said. "Think about it, Phil! A whole civilization has come and gone. The ebb and flow of life itself. Here people once lived and loved. Took simple nourishment. Worshipped the gods of their choice and lay down among the leaves in love. Nurtured their offspring and revered their old. In our busy world we have no time to think of such matters. It's go, go, go all the time. Make that sale and tote that bale. With nary a moment for reflection." He slipped the glasses back on his face. "It makes you realize how unimportant a single life is in the grand scheme of things."

"I happen to think," I said, "that a single life is damn important in the grand scheme of things, as you call it."

Off came the glasses again and Hacker looked at me quizzically. "Do you, Phil? Do you really think that?"

"Of course I do." I had listened to enough of his rubbish about civilizations and the ebb and flow of human life. "You're talking nonsense," I said. "The minute you start saying that a single life isn't important, you're on the road to barbarism. I expect every bloody dictator in history has justified his actions on the grounds that a single life isn't important in the grand scheme of things." Embarrassed by this uncharacteristic outburst, I looked away at the blue sky.

Hacker rubbed his jaw. "I hadn't thought of it in that light," he said. "You may be right, of course." He whistled tunelessly and then stopped. "I guess you've read a lot of books, haven't you?"

"Some," I said. "I wouldn't say a lot. But reading books has really nothing to do with it."

"What I can't understand," said Hacker, "is why an obviously intelligent and well-read man like you has to resort to sarcasm. I mean, repeating my phrase 'the grand scheme of things.' It seems to me that was uncalled for. What in fact I detected in your little speech was the tone of the prissy little schoolteacher. The little know-it-all with his captive classroom audience. That's the kind of tone that could well lead me to break the teeth in your head."

"Look, Ted," I said, "I don't think there's much point

in discussing this any longer. I'm not going to stand here and be threatened."

He quickly seized my elbow. "Now just a minute. Don't get your bowels in an uproar, as my dear old gramps used to say. I was, of course, joking. Your teeth are safe, pal."

"Please let go of my arm, Ted."

"Hush," he said. "Drink in the beauty of the scene. How many are vouchsafed a glimpse of the old Caribbean like this? What a storied past this great sea offers us! The fiery conquistadors with stout Cortez. The pirates who preyed on innocent cargo vessels. My guidebook says there are hundreds of shipwrecks hereabouts. I was thinking about putting on the old wetsuit and going down for a look. Perhaps tomorrow. Would you be interested, Phil?"

"No."

"It's fun," he said, putting his arm around my shoulder. "Of course, you have to know what you're doing. I was a frogman in Nam. In the marines. Another fellow and I, why, we once blew up a bargeful of Orientals on the Mekong. Not a pretty sight, I can assure you. But war is never pretty, and the lowly foot soldier must do unpleasant things or incur the ire of his superiors."

I was now convinced he was mad. "I didn't know you were in Vietnam," I said carefully.

"Oh my, yes," Hacker said. "But then, there are plenty of things you don't know about me, Phil." He hugged me. "Let's take a closer look at the old Caribbean in all its majesty."

"Now wait a minute, Ted, please. Heights make me dizzy." We were moving slowly forward.

"It's all in the imagination," said Hacker. "Simple mind over matter. In Parachute School they tell you to forget about it. My sergeant was from Georgia. What a mean young man he was! But he taught me not to worry about heights."

We were only a few feet from the terrible edge when Hacker stopped and released me. "Will you just look at that!" he exclaimed. "That's as pretty a sight as you could wish for." He then violently pushed me toward the edge. By a miracle I was able to grab the branch of a bush and avoid the plunge to my death.

From the other side of the bush I faced my tormentor. "I don't know what you're up to, Hacker," I cried. "The other night you tried to drown me. And now you've tried to push me off this cliff. I think you're ill, Ted. You need help."

Hacker placed both forefingers in the corners of his mouth and waggled his tongue. "Philip Bannister meets the madman of Tulum." He laughed.

I had to get past him, but as I feinted one way, he stopped his foolishness and moved with me. He was very quick on his feet. "I don't know what's got into you, old man," he said, "but I deny psychosis. Can't you take a joke?"

"None of this is very funny, Ted."

"So who's laughing?" he whispered, and in a hoarse voice sang,

I'm bidin' my time
'Cause that's the kind of guy I'm . . .

It was then that I saw Mr. Yoshimodo. He was standing near the temple wall fixing his handkerchief hat which had come apart in the wind. He also seemed absorbed by the spectacle of the large man jumping from side to side and the small man waving his arms for attention. "There's the man who took our pictures on the ferry," I said.

Hacker turned. "Well, bless my britches, so it is!" He waved. "How are you doin', fellah?" Mr. Yoshimodo stolidly continued to regard us while I scrambled past Hacker on trembling legs.

Fifteen

I was now determined to stay as far away as possible from this peculiar American couple. There would be no more passionate embraces in little stone rooms with Corky Hacker; her husband was clearly a dangerous man and I certainly intend to emphasize this at my trial next month. For the rest of my holiday I was going to avoid them, and, with that thought in mind, I made my way slowly down the temple steps, glancing back once to be sure that Hacker was not there to assist my descent with a push. But he was standing near the top taking a picture of the couple in blue.

I found Corky and Joan in front of one of the stalls; they were inspecting a rack of Indian dresses. I told them that I had had enough of the spooky ruins and was going up on the highway to await the bus. It would have been useless to tell them that Hacker had nearly killed me, especially as he was soon hurrying toward us. "Would you believe it, Corky?" he said. "I just met a couple from Omaha."

"Omaha!" said Corky. "Gee."

"Yep. It sure is a small world." He looked past the dresses at the Indian saleslady. "You girls going to buy any of those dresses? I'll bet they were made in Hong Kong."

"Philip has seen enough and wants to go," said Joan. "What do you think, Ted?"

Hacker dried his face with a handkerchief. "I think we've covered just about everything. And I agree with Phil. I think we should head out."

I was infuriated by his heartiness and, falling into an angry silence, I walked on ahead. Behind me the three of them chattered and laughed and I quickened my pace until I was out of earshot.

A small group of tourists stood by the edge of the main highway awaiting the next bus. No one seemed to know exactly when it would arrive, though a young woman who had been there before said the service was fairly regular. This information provoked a sharp laugh from an unkempt, bearded young man who sat on a large stone securing the straps of his bedroll and knapsack. Five minutes later Joan and the Hackers arrived. Hacker immediately went into the cantina nearby and returned with four bottles of Coca-Cola. He passed these to Joan and Corky before nudging me. "Coke, Phil?"

"No," I said.

Hacker shrugged and looked around before turning to a female child of seven or eight years who was standing beside her parents, a faded blonde woman with an angry stare and a beefy-looking man with bulging eyes and an old-fashioned crewcut now greying. There were tattoos on his forearms. Under the Mexican sky his heavy brutal face had turned the colour of meat. "Excuse me, folks," said Hacker. "I just happen to have an extra Coke. And I wonder . . . would you be offended if I offered it to your little girl?"

The pop-eyed man gave Hacker a doubtful look. "I guess it's all right."

Hacker handed the soft drink to the girl. "Say thank you, Nadine," said the woman. Her voice had a faint drawl.

"I'm not supposed to take things from strangers," said Nadine, taking the Coca-Cola.

"That's very true, Nadine," Hacker said. "But your mommy and daddy are right here so there's no harm done. However, the general principle is sound. Never accept favours from strangers when your parents aren't around. Okay?"

"Uh-huh," said the girl, looking up at Hacker, who now grinned and said to the man, "That little girl of yours is a real picture."

"Thank you," said the man gruffly.

"Just a picture," said Hacker. "Why, the girl has the face of an angel. I'll bet she could make it on TV." He turned to his wife. "Corky? Hasn't this little girl got it?"

"She's a doll," Corky said.

"Joan?" asked Hacker.

"A lovely child," said my hypocritical wife who dislikes children. Hacker looked at me. "Phil?" The child's father stared at me.

"Yes, very nice," I muttered. The child sucked Coca-Cola through a straw.

"You're darn right," said Hacker. "I'd say this little girl is going to go a long way. And I'll tell you something else. I'll bet she's as smart as she looks."

"Her last report was very good," said the mother.

"I'll just bet it was," said Hacker, now displaying several packages of chewing gum. He proceeded to pass these around. "How about you, Phil?" he asked. "Have a chaw?" I shook my head. I had turned away from them and was looking down the road in the hope of seeing something that would transport us from the hot dusty roadside. I felt my neck burn as Hacker said, "My friend has decided to sulk for the rest of the day."

"Is that a fact?" said the man with the bulging eyes. I sensed he was regarding me with dislike.

"Yes," said Hacker. "You see, he's in a bit of a snit."

"What's a snit?" said the little girl.

"I had a brother," said the man. "Gone now, God rest his soul. He used to get like that. There were nine of us of a family but only Elmer took to snits. Took after an uncle, according to my momma. This was in Arkansas. Rupert County."

"I know it well," Hacker said. "A great part of the Union. Wonderful people."

"Well," the man continued, "when Elmer took to sulkin', there wasn't nothin' for it but the woodshed." He chuckled mirthlessly. "'It's time for the woodshed, Elly,' my daddy used to say. 'Course, Elmer was just a kid. There ain't really no excuse for a grown man to go into a snit."

"What's a snit?" repeated the little girl.

"Now you hush, Nadine," said her mother.

I watched gratefully as a bus appeared down the road. With terrible farting noises it pulled to a stop before us and we boarded. Mr. Yoshimodo was the last to squeeze into the crowded vehicle. There were, however, seats near the back, and I slid into a window seat with Joan beside me. The Hackers were across the aisle behind the crewcutted man. His wife and daughter occupied the seat in front of Joan and me. The driver was the same surly fellow who had chauffeured us earlier in the day, and so again we barrelled down the highway in that noisy derelict SceniCruiser.

My window was one of the few not open, and from time to time I saw in the dusty glass my own glum reflection. Beside me Joan hummed some trashy show tune. Hacker had engaged the late Elmer's brother in conversation. The man's name was Trumble. He and his wife had won a bowling tournament and been awarded a week's vacation in Mexico. Hacker profusely congratulated the both of them on this achievement.

The daughter had now cranked herself around on the seat and, in the way of small, ill-mannered children, was staring at me. "Are you still in a snit?" she asked finally. Of course I said nothing to that. The others talked about a snowstorm that had struck the middle of America. Trumble had read about it in some paper. The St. Louis airport was closed and this was received as good news by everyone listening. Nadine Trumble, meanwhile, was making grotesque faces and once stuck her tongue out at me. Like small human monsters everywhere, she had perceived that I was a pariah and therefore could be insulted with impunity. The child had a very small head. I could easily have enclosed it in both my hands, and, staring at her foolish face, I enjoyed a pleasing fantasy of doing just that.

"Has the cat cut your tongue?" she asked.

Hacker interrupted Trumble. "Whoa! Hang on, Willard. Did you just hear what Nadine said?" He laughed. "I just heard that daughter of yours ask old Phil over there if the cat had cut his tongue. Isn't that cute?"

"Well, I just never," said Mrs. Trumble, giving her daughter a sour smile. "You just turn around there now."

"I don't want to," Nadine said.

"Can you beat it?" said her father.

"Oh, she's sharp as a tack, that's easy to tell," said Hacker. "Say, Phil, have you got an answer for her?"

I stared ahead and Joan dug her elbow into my side. "Philip? Ted's talking to you."

"I can hear him," I said.

Hacker leaned across the aisle and shouted. "Come on, Phil, old boy. She's just a child. It's only a joke."

"What's eatin' him, anyway?" asked Trumble.

Hacker laughed. "Oh, he lost his sand pail at the beach this afternoon. He's been sulking ever since."

The man looked over at me with hostility. "His sand pail, eh? That's a good one." He looked ready to punch me in the face.

"Did you really lose your sand pail?" asked his daughter.

"No, honey," said Joan, "but he might just as well have because he's behaving like a bad little boy."

I turned to Joan. "Will you kindly shut your mouth?"

Most of the passengers within earshot were now staring at us. "He just told her to shut her mouth," announced Nadine Trumble. Several people smiled, though Joan was not amused. The child had gone too far and Joan was now the displeased English lady on vacation. Her long face looked suddenly prim and stony with anger.

Hacker again leaned across the aisle to Nadine Trumble. "Isn't Phil a naughty widdle boy, Nadine?"

The child laughed delightedly. Looking out the window I saw something dark hurrying through the undergrowth. Was it a forest rat? A species of wild pig? In my mind's eye, I saw Hacker naked and secured to the ground by thick vines. Within the hour I would open both cages of starving beasts. In time the child exhausted her interest in me and went to sleep in her mother's lap. Other passengers, too, fell silent and nodded off as the bus rolled through the warm late afternoon.

It was dusk when we arrived at Playa del Carmen and tramped unhappily onto the little ferry. The talkative cheerfulness of the morning voyage had vanished, and many tourists now had the cranky, bitter look of persons who suspect they may have been swindled in some vague way by the travel agent's promise of extraordinary sights. Stomachs were empty and legs were tired. People stared out at the dark water and the receding lights of Playa del Carmen with eyes glazed by fatigue and sunlight. Corky Hacker smiled at me sadly. Subdued by the long day, we sat close together on the slatted wooden benches.

Nadine Trumble, however, seemed refreshed by her nap and, seated beside her parents, grew bored and fidgety. After a moment she got up and stood in front of me. "Has the cat still cut your tongue?" she asked, looking shyly at Hacker. Below us the ship's engines pounded away; you could feel the vibration through your shoes. "I said," repeated Nadine Trumble, "has the cat cut your tongue?"

On the other side of Joan, Hacker said loudly, "Listen, Trumble! Why won't you tell this brat of yours to knock it off?"

A few people gasped, but the Trumbles looked only

bewildered. Had they heard correctly? The man surely hadn't called their daughter a brat? But the child was dismayed and, looking at Hacker, said defiantly, "I am not a brat. My daddy is going to beat you up for saying that." She turned to her father. "Aren't you, Daddy?"

"You are so a brat," said Hacker. "You're a spoiled, rotten little brat with a big mouth and no manners. Go find the propeller to play with!"

"Hey!" said Trumble, his eyes bulging with outrage and terror.

"Hay for your horse, cracker," said the mad Nebraskan. "Want to make something out of it?"

"Willard!" said Trumble's wife, "Are you gonna let him talk that way about you?"

"Shut up," said Trumble in a fierce quiet voice. He was leaning forward, staring wildly at Hacker. He seemed to be swelling before our eyes like the hog-nosed viper when confronting enemies. I would not have been surprised to see the buttons explode from his shirt, exposing a brawny matted chest.

A crying Nadine buried her face in her mother's lap. From there she wailed, "I am not a brat. Make Daddy beat him up, please. Oh please, Mommy!"

"Oh Lordy!" cried Hacker in a tormented voice. "Take that squealing creature away from here!"

I looked over at him. He had covered his ears with his hands. "Is there any sound worse than a brat crying?" shouted Hacker. "I submit, ladies and gentlemen of the jury, there is not. Oh, take it away! Overboard with it, please!"

"Willaaaaaaaard!" Mrs. Trumble's voice was a cry of pain in the dark night. Even the Mexican families who had observed this commotion with impassive faces looked startled.

Willard Trumble stared at the four of us. He was not a coward; in fact, I guessed he was capable of great violence. But Hacker's preposterous behaviour had mesmerized him; Trumble had lost whatever confidence he might once have possessed and he could no longer deal with the situation. He dismissed the four of us with a wave of his hand. "You must be nuts," he said. "A bunch of dope fiends. You're prolly all nuts." He got up and walked to the railing, where his wife and child joined him. There they stood, looking out at the black water and whispering angrily among themselves.

I felt some sympathy for the bowler from Rupert County, Arkansas. No matter how much he enjoyed this week in Mexico, he would always remember those few humiliating moments on the ferry from Playa del Carmen. Hacker had contrived to ruin his holiday, too.

Sixteen

Lying in bed that night I decided to go home early, the next day in fact if I could book a flight. I was already tired of the island and the tourists. But mostly I was puzzled and frightened by the Hackers; I was growing more and more convinced (and how right my intuition was!) that some calamity lay waiting for anyone who ventured near them. When I conveyed my intentions to Joan, she only shrugged. Feelings between us were badly strained by the day's events. We had dined alone in an atmosphere of stiff courtesy ("Pass the salt, please . . . Thank you . . . May I have some of that sauce? . . . Of course, etc., etc.") often affected by persons who are furious with one another but too polite to come to blows.

After the chilly formality of this meal we returned to our hotel room. Joan complained of a headache and so placed herself before the dresser and made ghastly faces at the mirror. It was some kind of isometric nonsense that was supposed to relieve symptoms of neuralgia. I lay in bed sipping a whiskey and soda and glancing through an arresting volume on Victorian literature.

From her post in front of the mirror Joan said, "You can of course suit yourself, Philip. I think you've certainly demonstrated on this trip that you're not much fun anyway." I considered this observation unjust. I have always thought of myself as a good sport who is unafraid to don the cap and bells when the occasion demands. I have dressed as St. Nicholas and distributed gifts at the Budger House party. My costumes at the Pre-Lenten Revels have often provoked admiration; last year the theme was Great Figures in English Literature and I went as Justice Shallow. Many found it an interesting and original impersonation. I reminded Joan of this while she rubbed some cream into her face.

"You won't get a refund, you know," she said, tensing the muscles in her throat so that the cords stood out alarmingly. She looked to have aged in the two and a half years of our marriage. I decided she would look altogether grim at fifty; a leathery old trout who swam twenty lengths in the pool every morning.

"It's quite stupid to throw money away like that," she said. "If it were I, I should never hear the end of it."

"No, I don't suppose you should, should you," I replied, taking a little more whiskey. The drink tasted of liquorice but it was not unpleasant.

Joan rose and, hunching up her shoulders, rotated her head like a pugilist before a fight. I had seen her perform this exercise hundreds of times. To be civil I inquired about her headache.

"Not so bad now," she said, opening the small refrigerator and taking out a beer. After a long swallow she belched softly. Standing in her muumuu she looked suddenly dejected.

"What's the matter with you?" I asked.

"I was thinking of poor Dwight," she said. "What fun he was! And how he would have enjoyed this! He'd have written a poem for me. I remember so clearly the night he finished *Mrs. Donovan's Tiny Bird*."

I watched her go out to the balcony with her beer. A sentimental woman. Usually she maligned the dead poet; it was only when I was in bad odour that Tushy's ghost received these charitable reminiscences. I began to feel drowsy as I sipped my whiskey and read a chapter on the composition of Charles Kingsley's *The Water Babies*. This was a book I fondly remembered from my father's library; its illustrations of plump naked children had been erotically inspiring to my twelve-year-old sensibility. Make of that what you will, Doctor!

From a balcony nearby came the sounds of a party and I recognized the voices of Fred Flintstone and friends. I thought of Joan standing alone on the balcony with her memories. I called out to her. "Aren't you coming to bed?"

She belched again and said, "All in good time."

"Suit yourself," I said, falling almost immediately into a troubled sleep in which I dreamt of serpents.

I place no great value on the analysis of dreams. The landscape of sleep is mysterious terrain, and in his slumbers the traveller may behold many wonderful or repellent sights that deft explanation. Yet it is a fact that some of us benighted voyagers return in our dreams to images both loathsome and terrifying. Like De Quincey with his recurring nightmare of Chinamen and crocodiles, I frequently dream of great dark serpents that want to eat me. After a visit from these beasts, I wake up and lie staring into the darkness for an hour.

And this is what I thought I did on that Tuesday night in the El Gringo Hotel. I remember lying on the narrow bed, listening to the palm fronds as they crackled in the wind from the sea. But I cannot recall my eyes opening, and, stranger intelligence yet, I thought I heard the voices of my wife and Corky Hacker. They seemed to be near my bed and they were laughing softly and whispering. But since I did not see them, I concluded the next morning that I had never awakened, but had only dreamed of their whispers and laughter.

Seventeen

On Wednesday morning I arose with a severe headache. The room was bright with sunshine. Joan was already up and in the shower singing some catchpenny tune from a Broadway show. I was still determined to leave Mexico that day and indeed phoned the airline office and talked to a helpful woman who informed me that there was a seat available on a flight that afternoon. She advised me to book at once. Out of decency I intended to cash my travellers' cheques at the hotel and give the money to Joan. Thus I asked the airline lady if I could pay for my ticket with a credit card. She told me this was satisfactory and asked for the number. When I opened my billfold I discovered that all my credit cards were missing along with the travellers' cheques. There remained only a twenty-dollar bill. I told the clerk I would phone back and began a frantic search through my clothes.

I was busy at this when Joan came out of the bathroom wearing her muumuu. On her head was a large hotel towel fashioned into a sort of turban. By then I was on my hands and knees exploring the floor of the wardrobe. "What on earth are you doing?" asked Joan, looking down at me.

"I'm looking for my credit cards and money. They're not in my billfold." I was beginning to submit to the panic that must assail all travellers who suddenly find themselves without funds in a foreign land. I looked up at my wife. "Perhaps you've forgotten, but I meant what I said last night. I'm catching an afternoon flight home. They are keeping a seat for me. All I have to do now is provide them with a credit card number. Will you get me some aspirin before my head falls off?"

"Darling, why are you carrying on like this? We've only another few days. What can it matter?" She went off to the bathroom and returned with aspirin and a glass of mineral water. I swallowed the medicine on my knees. "If you'd just give the place half a chance," said Joan. "You're such a fusspot. The old Gannymedian. You must learn to relax when you visit another part of the world. I know you find the Hackers a bit unconventional, but I must confess I find them bracing." She lit a cigarette. "After all, why travel if you aren't prepared to be challenged and enjoy people who are different?"

I got to my feet. "I don't mind people who are different, but I object to consorting with a man who is obviously deranged. And who, moreover, seems to have it in for me, God knows why."

"That's utter nonsense. Ted's very fond of you and has said so to me. I don't know where you get these ridiculous ideas."

"Ridiculous or no, I'm going home. You can stay for the rest of the week and the best of British luck to you and the couple from Lincoln. If I can just find my bloody money!"

"Speaking of money," said Joan, "don't you think this little whim of yours is a frightful waste when our return fare is already paid for? Saturday is only three days away, for heaven's sake. You're always scolding *me* about money."

I rezippered the valises and looked about the room. "And how," continued Joan, "will it look at the school? Your turning up a few days early, I mean? Tongues will wag, I shouldn't wonder."

"Let them wag and let them wonder," I said, examining the dresser drawers.

"Such a lot of busybodies," said Joan. "Always inventing stories. Mona Murdoch will have me running off with a blackamoor."

"It couldn't have been a pickpocket," I said. "A pickpocket wouldn't take the cards and put the billfold *back* in my jacket. And I distinctly remember having the money before I retired last night. I stood by this very dresser counting it. You saw me, Joan. I'm always very careful about money when I'm travelling. I always look after the boys' money on the cricket tours. I am *not* careless about money. This is utterly maddening."

"Well, there is no reason to *rave*, darling."

"The only explanation," I said, "is an intruder. Doubtless from the balcony. A cat burglar, as they're sometimes called. I expect you left the balcony door open last night and a prowler got in. Are you missing anything, by the way? Have you checked your purse?" I was beginning to perspire in the air-conditioned room.

Joan sat on her bed and began to paint her toenails. With her leg up, the muumuu fell open, affording me a glimpse of her parts. But where was my money? Her air of indifference infuriated me. "Damn it, are you going to sit there decorating your feet while I repeat that all my funds have been stolen?"

"Oh, Philip, please don't carry on so," she said. "I have *my* cards and about a hundred in cash. It's only three more days. We'll manage."

I sat on my bed, dispirited by this sudden intrusion of disorder. Now I would have to get in touch with the various credit card agencies and alert the people who dealt in travellers' cheques. Was there a Cooks office in the village? I wondered. Could I, for that matter, lay my hands on the numbers of the cheques? Perhaps much the best thing would be to explain my predicament to the local bank manager. Surely he would be sympathetic; such knavery must be commonplace on a resort island, though it was probably ingenuous on my part to expect a native to admit as much.

Sitting on the bed with these burdensome thoughts, I recalled Neddy Blake's remark that early in life he'd found travelling such a horror that he now went nowhere except Great Toe Lake in August.

"I'm going to phone the bank," I said, "and ask to see the manager. Explain the situation. Have them at least aware of things before the scoundrel spends me into the poorhouse."

"I shouldn't bother if I were you," said Joan, finishing her toenails.

"Why ever not, may I ask?"

"Because, darling, I'm the scoundrel. I took your boffy old credit cards and travellers' cheques." She smiled brilliantly at me.

"Why, for heaven's sake?"

"Oh, Philip," she said, getting up and coming over to me. "Don't let's argue. We're on holidays and I'm having such a good time. You don't want to leave today and spoil my good time, do you?"

"Nonsense," I said, standing up. "I can't see your missing me at all. You spend most of your time with the Hackers. And that reminds me. We haven't yet thrashed that out. I am, of course, referring to the other night and what happened after that revolting game."

Joan placed her arms around my neck. "But, my precious, there's nothing to thrash out. Now listen to me! The Hackers are just wayfarers on the path of life. A companionable couple whom the Fates have decreed must enter our lives for a mere week. But their presence is but a trifle. *A bagatelle!* Ted's a boor, you're quite right about that. And Corky is unquestionably a little simp with her 'Oh Teddy' routine. Not to mention her 'Gee, I didn't know that' stuff. The little lady is not as innocent as she would have us believe. But what of it, my pet? Why make such a fuss over two people we'll never see again after Saturday?" She pressed herself against me. "Promise you won't go back today."

"Give me back my credit cards and travellers' cheques, Joan! Where have you put them, damn it?"

She bit my earlobe. "Let's have a quickie!"

During the first months of our marriage, such playfulness was alluring, and often, like creatures of the wild, we chased each other naked around my apartment. I am certain that the boys of Budger House heard our cries of delight, and inspired, crept off to their mattresses to grasp a beggar's bliss. Now, however, I found such tactics distressingly coy. Joan tightened her grip on my neck. "Come on, big boy. Give it to me! Let's have a go."

I disengaged her arms from my neck. "I shall tell you the truth, Joan. I am not overjoyed by the news that you rifled my billfold last night while I lay sleeping. Such an action, it seems to me, opens a basic breach in the relationship. And now, for the last time, may I have my documents?"

Joan stepped back and, opening her muumuu, revealed her various treasures. Performing a shimmy she whispered, "Sock it to me, baby, eight to the bar!"

"Stop this foolishness, Joan, and tell me where you've put my cards." Beating her was out of the question for, although I am a murderer, I am not a man of violence.

She closed the garment and made a little grimace. "I think you're an utter beast, Philip. If poor Dwight were here, he would have had me by now. He was an *artist*."

I groaned. "Dwight again."

"He'd have called me his doxy and, throwing me on the bed, thrust home. While you deny me my lawful marital rights." She removed the turban and shook out her long hair. At the knocking on the door she raised her head. "Hark! A visitor!" And like Ophelia, she ran barefoot to the door. Had she been drinking? I wondered. I hadn't smelled it on her, nor could I remember her taking alcohol this early in the day.

She returned with Corky Hacker who was wearing a white tank top and pleated skirt. With her hair enclosed in a headband she looked like a tennis player. "Hi everyone," she said brightly.

"I'm not quite ready yet, my dear," said Joan, "but I shan't be a minute." She began to rummage in the wardrobe while Corky Hacker sat down on the bed beside me. Her taffy-coloured thighs felt warm against my leg. How had she managed such a wonderful tan in just a few days? I wondered.

"And how are you this morning, Philip?" she asked.

It didn't seem worth explaining about the purloined money and my plans to leave early, so I merely mumbled greetings. "Ted's already in the water," she said.

Like a customer in a dress shop, Joan was inspecting a blouse. "Ted was hoping you'd join him this morning, Philip," said Corky. "He thought you might get a kick out of it."

"I'm afraid I'm indifferent to scuba diving or whatever you call it. And I very much doubt whether I could keep up with a former frogman."

Corky Hacker looked puzzled. "Who's a former frogman?"

"Why, your husband, of course," I said. "He told me he was a frogman in the marines in Vietnam."

Corky Hacker made her instinctive gesture of astonishment, a hand clapped over her mouth to repel an explosion of laughter. "Ted said that? Oh, he was just pulling your leg, Philip. Ted was never in the marines. The draft board rejected him during the Vietnam thing. He's 4-F, poor guy. It has something to do with his heart. He told me all about it before we were engaged. He said at the time that it was up to me whether I wanted to marry someone with a bum ticker. That's what he calls it, his bum ticker. Of course I said it didn't make any difference to me, because I was so head over heels in love with the big galoot. But it was so sweet of him to tell me. However, that's Ted for you."

"Yes," I said, "that's Ted for you." I never realized

how much I hated the man. "And I suppose he never went to medical school either?"

"Medical school?" She laughed. Joan had gone into the bathroom. Corky shook her lovely head. "Ted in medical school? Did he really tell you that? Why, if you cut your finger, Ted nearly passes out. He can't stand the sight of blood."

She was absently knocking those brown biscuits of knees together and I felt a surge of lust.

"What did you mean in that little room in Tulum yesterday?" I whispered. "About being careful? 'We must be careful,' you said. Were you referring to your husband's jealousy?"

She smiled at me and put a finger to her lips as Joan came out of the bathroom. Her mouth was white with dentifrice and she was holding a toothbrush and a glass. She spoke through the white stuff. "Who can't stand the sight of blood?"

"Teddy, of course," said Corky. "He's been pulling Philip's leg again. Going on about being in the marines and then in medical school." She sighed heavily. "Poor Teddy! It's just his way of compensating. He's only a salesman for Big Pharmaceutical. Just a sweet, insecure guy who now and again fantasizes about being strong and popular and famous."

"I could see that right away," said Joan, brushing her teeth. She stopped and dipped the toothbrush into the glass of mineral water. "Ted is basically a very gentle human. He reminds me of my late husband Dwight Tushy. Another big, gentle man. Remember I told you about Dwight? The poet?

Was it worth pointing out, I wondered, the number of

times Joan had related to me how a drunken Dwight Tushy had beaten her black and blue?

"There's poetry in Ted, too," said Corky Hacker. "He's shown me some stuff he's written. He writes it sometimes when he's travelling for Big. In an airport lounge maybe on a Sunday afternoon. He wrote one poem about Mom Hacker and I couldn't help it. It just made me cry."

"Ted has the same sweet nature as poor Dwight," said Joan. "But basically he's insecure. Dwight was very insecure. In spite of his talent."

"That's it," said Corky, "the insecurity."

"Like frightened little boys on the playground," said Joan. "It's five o'clock on a winter afternoon. It's getting dark and everyone else has gone home."

"God, yes. Exactly."

Joan went to the bathroom and we heard her expectorate into the washbasin. When she returned she said to me, "And what are your plans for today, my love? I shouldn't think you'd want to come shopping with Corky and me?"

"I haven't any money, remember."

Joan smiled. "It's probably just as well. It'll be mostly girl talk. Surely you and Ted can find something to do while we ladies go into town."

"Sure they can," said Corky. "There's a putt-putt golf course just down the road. And the hotel has a games room in the basement with Ping-Pong and a pool table."

Joan was now laying out her day's clothes on the bed. "I'm just running out of things to wear," she said helplessly. "I didn't bring nearly enough," she added, glancing at Corky Hacker. "And you always look so smashing." Corky flushed. "That outfit you're wearing, for instance," said Joan. "It's perfectly stunning."

Corky stood up. "Oh! Do you like it? It's really a combination swim-and-beach thing. See!" She unbuttoned the skirt to display a three-inch strip of material, panties of a sort, I suppose; it barely covered her fork. "Cute isn't it?" she said, turning like a fashion model. Joan and I both appraised Corky Hacker's luscious lower half.

"It's really something," Joan said in a hoarse voice.

"Thanks," said Corky, rebuttoning the skirt and watching as Joan stepped *naked* from her muumuu. She began to sort through the clothes on the bed.

I have spent my life among adolescent boys and so I cannot pretend to understand the female mentality. Do women who have known one another only a few days undress in front of each other like men in a locker room? It seemed very odd to me, the more so when you consider that I was present.

"You've certainly kept your figure, Joan," said Corky.

"Why, thank you, my dear," said Joan, simpering a little. "I suspect Philip thinks my breasts are too large."

"Oh no," Corky said. "They're not. They're just right." She hesitated. "I wish I were . . . a little better endowed."

"Nonsense," said Joan. "You're perfect just as you are."

She fastened a brassiere over those enormous globes and climbed into a pair of tailored slacks. It was rather like a striptease in reverse. Corky Hacker continued to gaze fixedly as Joan buttoned a severe-looking black-and-white striped shirt. There followed a maroon necktie which she knotted carefully at her throat. I could form no accurate memory of having seen her before in such garb.

"I love your hair," said Corky. "I wish I could wear mine straight. But it's just naturally curly. It's sure limiting style-wise."

"You should not spend one moment worrying your pretty head over such minutiae," said Joan, striding across the room in this Joan Crawford I-mean-business outfit. Sitting in front of the mirror she began to pull a tortoiseshell brush through her hair.

"Oh, let me, please," cried Corky, taking the brush and standing behind my wife.

I took this opportunity to seize Joan's handbag. As I searched through it, she looked sideways at me. She seemed amused. "I should very much doubt, Philip, whether there is anything in my handbag that would be of the remotest interest to you."

"Is that so?" I had, of course, hoped to extract her credit cards and currency. But there was no wallet; all I found was the usual detritus of a woman's handbag: comb, compact, tissues, cigarettes, emery boards, keys, etc.

"Joan," I explained to Corky, "is playing a little game on me. She's taken all my money."

"Oh, Teddy and I play little games like that all the time. It's all part of married life." She had expertly worked my wife's hair into a bun arrangement at the back. "There! How's that?"

"It's absolutely perfect, my dear," said Joan, inspecting her person. "Thanks so much."

Where, I wondered, could Joan be keeping not only my

money but her own? The tailored pants admitted no posterior bulge where a wallet might be concealed. There was only a single pocket in the shirt and it was empty. Joan stood up and pecked my cheek. "We're off, precious heart. Have a nice day. I should think we'll be back well in time for drinkees! Say, five o'clock!"

"We're going to make a day of it," said Corky Hacker, excited as a child. She wagged a finger at me and looked stern. "Now you and Teddy behave yourselves, Philip. There are some darn attractive girls staying at this hotel. I saw a couple of airline stewardesses at breakfast. Wow, are they dolls!"

"Oh tut," said Joan. "Let the boys enjoy a carefree day if they so desire. They are, after all, on holidays."

Corky Hacker winked at me. "Well, just remember then, if you can't be good, be careful."

"Yes," said Joan, picking up her handbag, "the old caveat 'wear armour' still holds true. See you anon, my darling."

After they left I began to search the room. I looked everywhere and found only a solitary peso under the bed. In fact, I was on my hands and knees when the door opened and Hacker looked in. "Have they gone, Phil?" he asked.

"Yes," I said dully.

He entered smiling.

Eighteen

Hacker had just come from the sea. His hair was still plastered to his head and water dripped from his legs. He wore only the horrid net swimming trunks and an old grey sweatshirt upon which was stencilled the word *Nebraska*. I quickly got to my feet as he walked across the room and sat down. His damp, heavy codpiece hung over the edge of the bed. "I hope you'll excuse the informal attire, Phil," he said.

"Our wives have gone into town shopping," I replied. He nodded. "They suggested that we might do something together, but I'm rather behind in my reading, you see, and . . ." I stopped, unsettled by Hacker's expression of benign perplexity. It was the same puzzled stare worn by students who sat listening while I enumerated the reasons behind their low grades. But the silence between us deepened and became awkward. I sat on the chair opposite him and said, "Look Ted. Perhaps we both got off on the wrong foot. I will confess that I was fed up enough just an hour ago to want to go home. But . . . well, that's another story. Now, I've no wish to hurt your feelings, but I can't see that we have much in common. Your wife mentioned a games room, but I'm not much for billiards or table tennis. Cricket is about the only game I can manage. What I'm suggesting is, and I'm sorry if I'm putting it badly, but well, damn it, I'd prefer to be alone today and read."

Hacker clasped his hands together and, peering down at them, rotated his thumbs. He looked thoughtful and I saw the youth in him. With such a look he must surely have winkled out a B minus from a sympathetic French teacher. "I'm sorry," I lied, "and I certainly hope you don't take any of this personally. It's simply a matter of different backgrounds, different customs, different interests, different tastes. Not better, mind you, just different. Oh, I expect you must find me a bit unusual and perhaps I am. After all those years in a boarding school, I suppose I am something of a queer old fish. . . ."

Hacker looked up, brightening. "You are?"

"What?"

He rested his hands on his knees and, clearing his throat, said, "Phil, there's something I've been meaning to ask you, and I hope you won't take the query amiss."

I experience a sharp sense of unease as Hacker looked at the ceiling and abruptly laughed. "Oh boy, this is hard! This is a tough mother." He leaned forward and frowned. "Do you know, Phil, this reminds me a little of my old football days at college. After the practices, you'd have a shower and then sit around and shoot the breeze with some of the guys. One by one people would drift out and then there'd be the final bang of a locker door. The smell of liniment. The shouts from the playing field. Perhaps the smell of burning leaves coming through an open window. You'd sit there wearing maybe only . . . towels." He cleared his throat again. "Those intimate times remain for me among my sweetest memories."

"What did you want to ask me, Ted?" I didn't care for

Hacker in these moods of sentimentality; they nearly always presaged violence.

"How long have you been teaching at that boys' school, Phil?"

"At The Gannymede? Well, let me see. It's twenty-three years now. Nearly a quarter of a century."

Hacker shook his head. "Imagine. Nearly a quarter of a century at a boys' school!"

"Well, and of course before that I was a student. Except for four years at university, The Gannymede has really been my life."

"There's something really beautiful about young men, isn't there, Phil? It's almost inspiring. Of course, I never had a private education. Dad was just a bus driver. But there was a private school on the other side of town. Lindhaven Academy. Sometimes we played exhibition games against them. Golly, they were clean-cut, pleasant fellows. Always so nicely turned out. Oh, some of the oafs I went to school with used to make fun of that. But secretly I admired them. Admired their shirts and ties and blazers. Their haircuts. Their *savoir faire*." Hacker looked closely at me. "They were beautiful young men." He paused. "And I'll bet you've seen some beautiful young men in your time, Phil."

"Well . . ."

Hacker stood up suddenly. "I was once considered beautiful in my own right. During my first year of college I earned a few ducats by posing for students over at the art school. I turned not a few heads in my day, Phil. And I'm still not in bad shape." Crossing his arms in front of him he quickly pulled his sweatshirt over his head and, casting it aside, flexed his muscles and gazed across the room.

"What do you think?" he asked.

"Ted, I think it's unnecessary to do that."

"I was one ninety-eight in those days. I'm only two hundred and ten now. That's not bad."

"Please stop posing, Ted. It's embarrassing."

He expelled his breath and relaxed his muscles. Then, picking up his sweatshirt, he tied the sleeves around his neck and walked across the room shaking his head. Standing by the window he said, "Boy, you're a cool one! I've got to hand it to you, Phil, you sure know how to control yourself."

"What in heaven's name are you talking about?"

He walked back and stood over me. "All right, darn it, I'll grasp the nettle. Cross your heart and hope to die if, in all those years at that school, you never lusted after a boy. A beautiful firm youth with golden locks. Or perhaps a sable-haired youngster with dark lustrous eyes and a hit of the sensuous Mediterranean about him."

"Now look, Hacker," I cried, "I've endured these suspicions all my life."

He smiled down at me. "There's no shame in it, Phil. We have appetites like everyone else. There's nothing *dirty* about it, for the love of Pete. Think of the Greeks and their glorious contribution to our civilization. Consider the great artists down through the centuries. Michaelangelo, of course, comes to mind. Shakespeare, too, it seems . . ."

"Whatever you may think, Hacker," I said, "I am not . . . I have nothing against it, mind you. Naturally, a boarding school is out of the question for such a person. A certain element of trust is assumed. The scandal alone . . ."

Hacker seemed not to be listening as his fierce blue eyes gazed past me. "I've dreamt of a civilized friendship with an older man," he said. "Someone quiet and reserved. Dignified. A smoker of briars and a reader of weighty volumes." He smiled at me. "I'm lonely, Phil. You don't know what it's like working for Big. Every month there are sales quotas to meet. Computer printouts locating target areas for our liver pills and hemorrhoid salves. Those machines are merciless with underachievers. And then there are the snotty doctors. Some of the females are awful. Advances are sometimes made. Oh, the vulgarity of commerce is so depressing! There is a pediatrician in St. Paul who will not write prescriptions for Big's products unless I allow her to put a hand on my erect member. These are the little burdens I carry about with me, Phil. And no one knows or asks or seems to care."

"I'm sorry."

"And then there are the lonely nights in the hotels. The bars are always filled with chippies, and so you go to your room and face the loneliness of another night on the road. You've probably never stood by a hotel window at three o'clock in the morning looking down as the neon lights blink on the wet pavement. From the bar down the street you can hear the lonely wail of the saxophone. So you stand there behind the venetian blinds, and stare down at the empty glass in your hand and wonder where your life is going." He paused. "Don't you see, Phil? I need companionship and a lasting, meaningful relationship."

"But you're married to a beautiful woman!" I said.

He shook his head knowingly. "Oh, I am, I know I am. You're right, of course, and God bless the Cork. She's everything a fellah could ask for in a wife. But I put it to you, Phil . . . Can't a person want more? Life offers several cups of wine to be savoured and it behooves us to drink."

Hacker began to pace back and forth in front of me. "Why, we could read poetry together, you and I! Gosh, I remember from college. English 001. A. H. Clough.

Say not the struggle not availeth
the labour and the wounds are vain.

I never understood what those lines meant. For that matter, I still don't. But you're an English teacher, Phil, and you could help me. I'm not the insensitive swine you take me for. I have feelings. I admire beauty. The falling leaves of October. The sleeping face. I saw Swan Lake once. *Adored* it! Then there are sunsets and Christmas." He began to sing.

Chestnuts roasting on the open fire
Jackdaws nipping your nose.

"Don't you mean 'Jack Frost nipping at your nose'?" I asked.

Hacker stopped pacing and stared at me. "What?"

"It's not important, Ted, forget it."

"No, please. What did you just say?"

"It's not really important. It's the old pedantic schoolteacher in me rising to the surface."

He continued to stare at me. "Did I say something wrong?"

"Well, you misquoted the lyrics of the song, Ted. I believe it's 'Jack Frost nipping at your nose.'"

"It is?"

"Yes."

"Well, for goodness sakes. And all these years I thought it was jackdaws." He grasped the sleeves of the sweatshirt. He looked abject. "What's a jackdaw, by the way?"

"It's a bird," I said. "A kind of crow. A grackle."

"A grackle," he said, astonished. "A grackle nipping at your nose! Well, of course, that makes no sense at all, does it?" He laughed bitterly. "Isn't that just typical of me? Do you see what I mean, Phil? That's so much the kind of thing I was referring to! Oh God, there's so much I don't know!"

He began to pace again, then suddenly broke toward me and knelt in front of my chair. "But I'm willing to learn. I need a patient teacher though." He grinned. "Meanwhile, how about a little kiss?"

"Ted, please. This has surely gone too far."

"Remember that old hit from the war years? Before my time, of course, but I can remember my mom singing it in the kitchen while she baked a cake." He began to sing in a husky voice.

Give me a little kiss, will you huh?
And I'll give it right back to you!

I surprised him by bolting from my chair; I'm sure he

wasn't prepared for such quickness in a man of my years. And so I left him kneeling in front of the empty chair from where he smiled gently at me. "Okay, Phil, I'm not dense. I can take a hint. But you can't blame a guy for trying." He got up and put on his sweatshirt. "Perhaps," he said, walking stiffly toward the door, "I committed an indiscretion. Who knows, in this cynical, topsy-turvy world where Hatred is a constant and Love is always suspect? I suppose I assumed that with your experience in that boarding school, you would at least be *simpatico*."

Before leaving he stopped and looked back at me. "Phil, I trust you won't mention this unhappy little interlude to my wife. I am at your mercy, of course, but I'm counting on the maturity and good judgment of your years. See you later, pal," he added softly, closing the door behind him.

Nineteen

Very well, madam, I will get on with the orgy and the murders. But allow me first to record sad tidings from the Land of Smiles. These arrived today on the facility's stationery over the grim-looking signature of one Grace Welch, R.N., Supervisor.

Ms. Welch informs me that my dear aunts have *both* succumbed to senile dementia and may now be considered *non compos mentis*. It seems they do not comprehend my predicament, and are even unclear about my existence. Isn't it curious how both would descend into madness within the same week! But perhaps not so curious, for one sometimes hears of lifelong companions who expire within days of each other. I mention these family matter since they may have some bearing on the outcome of my trial next month.

In her last paragraph Ms. Welch, besides offering me the institution's chilly condolences, mentions the fact that my aunts' account is in arrears. Ms. Welch has written to Ross Parry about the matter, and his reply included the unhappy news that my aunts' estate has withered badly in recent years. In his letter, Parry rather insolently invited Ms. Welch to stand at the end of a long line of creditors. In the circumstances, the supervisor wonders whether I am prepared to assume the financial burden of my aunts' care. There is, of course, nothing I would assume more gladly, though I'm afraid there is precious little in the mutual account that my late wife ravished so thoroughly every month.

Money, alas, is always a problem, isn't it? And now I shall not receive further money orders from my aunts. And will old Miguel still offer his services and company gratis? Will I continue to enjoy the fresh fruit and the remnants of Miss Dodge's library? I suspect it would take an optimist of Panglossian dimension to be hopeful. And what of my *abrogado* Mr. Gomez who, when I think of it, mentioned money on his last visit? It seems Thrust and Parry has been dilatory in its correspondence with Mr. Gomez, and the good man reminded me that there are considerable expenses involved in my particular case. I said I understood perfectly, but was at a lost for suggestions.

I am beginning to entertain doubts about Ross Parry. We've never liked one another. I once gave a favourite nephew of his, a witless boy, a charitable D. On Prize Day, Parry, in some limp attempt at irony, made passing reference to how difficult it had become at The Gannymede to pass courses in "poetry and stuff." Dare I risk libel and suggest that Parry is engaged in some thimble-riggery that will deprive me of my inheritance?

Oh, sir, be patient! I shall be dwelling soon enough on the exotic subjects of sex and death. Pray let me linger a trifle longer over more prosaic matters. I have in my hands a letter from Neddy Blake who, in the fine tradition of Anglican clergymen, invites me to gird my loins for the days ahead. Neddy writes to say that Captain

Hale is taking the first eleven to England in July. Accompanying him this year will be young Evans, a Welshman and science master. How I shall miss the spires of Pook Hill School! And tea and biscuits in the gazebo at St. Harry's! Shall I ever again experience the thrill of seeing one of our batsmen cut to square leg four?

Mrs. Neddy has finally produced her long-awaited chapbook. *Chapel Flower Arranging for All Occasions* has been privately printed and is now on sale through the Women's Guild. My old enemy Milo Murdoch has been appointed assistant headmaster, a posting I find well-nigh incomprehensible. It puts me in mind of familiar words from the *Book of Common Prayer*. "I myself have seen the ungodly in great power, and flourishing like a green-bay tree."

Ralph Hotchkiss, hockey captain and eighteen-year-old fornicator, was expelled during the last week of the Lent Term along with five teammates. Something to do with narcotics. More to the point, however, comes the news that the faculty held a meeting chaired by the new assistant headmaster to discuss "the Bannister case." My colleagues busied themselves with the question of what exactly the school's position should be in the circumstances. It was generally agreed that considerable damage had been done to The Gannymede's reputation, and that further involvement might well lead to an "enrollment shortfall." How quickly and easily these ghastly new terms fall from the lips of the innocent!

Bea Corcoran, God bless her, offered to attend my trial in the capacity of character witness, provided that the school assume her expenses. This proposal was debated at some length and the motion for the funds narrowly defeated. I would give a month of what remains of my life for the names of those who voted on the nay side of that motion. It was decided, however, that those who wished to do so could send letters attesting to my good character to Mr. Gomez in Mexico City.

Miguel has just brought me some fruit, and I have promised to read to him from *The Cloister and the Hearth*, a book I heartily recommend to those of you who, like myself, are thoroughly fed up with the times in which we live.

Twenty

Let us now, as pleaders before the bench might phrase it, return to that fateful day. Or rather to the day before the fateful day; namely, the day I spurned Ted Hacker's absurd advances. I was, of course, shaken by that experience, and felt no guilt whatsoever in consuming a large vodka and tomato juice with my breakfast. I then went to the swimming pool which was empty except for Mr. Yoshimodo. He was gliding face down through the green water, his arms and legs opening and closing like those of some immense frog.

Later the robot salesman and I sat in the deck chairs by the pool and chatted. Throughout the conversation, we maintained an air of friendly reserve becoming gentlemen who suspect one another of being homosexual. Mr. Yoshimodo talked about his wife and children in Kobe and of how he missed the simple pleasures of the family. In response, I hastily invented a preposterous collection of virtues for my wife. We bought each other martinis, and expressed the hope that we would both live to see more cooperation, better cultural ties, increased trade, etc., etc., between the West and the Orient. Neither of us, I'm sure, believed a word of it.

Over lunch on the patio, I listened to a lecture on the robotization of industry. An hour later I staggered away, torpid from too much alcohol and food, and bewildered by the pitiless sunlight and a dystopian vision of mechanical contrivances fashioned from some new alloy that won't stain, tarnish, talk back, or bag at the knees. In my room I surrendered to the luxurious and silent embrace of the siesta, one of the few sensible ideas to emerge from hot climates.

I slept the livelong day and awakened stupefied. It was dark and I lay on the bed, listening to the surf beat against the shore. A powerful wind was blowing off the sea, and beyond my window the palm fronds rattled in the dark air. When I got up and went to the balcony, this strong fresh wind revived me. Below, the empty swimming pool glimmered greenly in the light from the hotel. The beach was deserted. From time to time lightning limned heavy clouds over the sea. Standing there in the windy black night I wondered what had become of Joan. It was nearly nine o'clock and she had been gone now for over ten hours. Or had she returned and, seeing me asleep, left again? And was she now up to fresh shenanigans with the singular Hackers? I set aside these questions while I bathed and dressed for dinner. I would dine alone with my book on the Victorians.

On my way to the dining room, I caught sight of the sadly dignified middle-aged gent in the lobby mirror. Joan was right; in my double-breasted blazer and flannels I did resemble the late Clifton Webb. In a few years I would be a spare elderly man with dry palms and a handkerchief tucked up my coat sleeve. My dear dead father, in fact.

At the front of the hotel Fred Flintstone and friends were bibulously trying to cram themselves into a taxi. Fred and I waved to each other before he was pulled into the back seat. The taxi roared off into the foolishly melodramatic night. Behind the desk the sallow clerk slept over his newspaper.

Dinner was a bizarre and melancholy hour. I was the only patron in the vast room. Where were the other guests? I decided that, like the Flintstones, most people had gone into town for the evening. It was not really so surprising as the hotel's food was appalling. The headwaiter fussed over me while his underlings brought dish after unsatisfactory dish. The hospital orderlies appeared with their guitars and, standing over me, strummed songs of love, I imagine. The older man had a gold tooth which gleamed when he smiled. Once he impertinently winked at me. Outside the gloomy wind pressed against the glass and the sea broke across the old wooden jetty. I felt haunted and unutterably lonely. Not even the confident Victorians helped.

Like some character in a story by Poe, I was assailed by dread, captive to some peculiar estrangement. Leaving my dinner half-finished, no great loss, I fled the dining room. I felt a sudden and desperate need for company. Why had I not run out to that taxi and asked Fred if he could squeeze me into the back seat with the others? Now, there is doubtless some psychological palaver that covers the condition I am trying to describe: something to do with a person who has lived all his years in a communal setting (the shuffle and cough of morning prayers, boisterous meals in Bung Hall, etc.) suddenly finding himself alone in a foreign land. A tourist, so to speak, with nothing to tour.

The Hackers' room was on the floor above us; this information I received from the desk clerk, who briefly roused himself to impart it. As I walked along the open balcony past darkened rooms, gusts of wind flayed the vines of bougainvillea and the bushes of hibiscus. In the jungle across the highway a bird screeched hideously. The Hackers' room was in darkness but the door was open, and from within came the gimcrack sounds of a mariachi band. By the open door I stood listening.

The music came from a radio, and soon the announcer spoke quickly in Spanish. The words *Coca-Cola* were repeated several times, and then his gibberish was followed by the voices of two men singing to the accompaniment of their blasted guitars. It was the same song I had left behind in the dining room. I knocked on the door. "Hullo there," I called. "Anyone home? Are you in there, Ted? Joan? Corky? It is I, Philip!"

There was no reply. Only the falsetto voices of the singers and the severe black wind playing havoc with the vegetation. Leaning into the room I called again. "Hullo, Hacker? Bannister here! Are Joan and Corky with you? I'm getting rather worried. Haven't seen them since this morning."

I wondered if perhaps he was asleep, and so stepped into the room, conscious of yet another shameless bit of melodramatic staging: the sea wind billowing the curtains by the open window, and from the darkness beyond, faraway muffled thunder. But the room seemed empty.

I turned to leave, when something blunt was thrust into the small of my back. "Spread 'em and freeze!" said a harsh voice.

"Now listen, Ted . . ."

"Up against the wall and legs apart," he said, pushing

me forward. "The weapon is in direct contact with your lower spine. It's pointed at an intricate network of nerves. One false move and you can forget about your evening stroll with old Shep. You can say goodbye to walks for charity, and hello Wheelchair City!"

"Please, Ted."

"Shut up and spread those legs!"

He rudely spread-eagled me against the wall and began to pat my trouser legs. I believe, in detective fiction, the term is *frisking*.

"Ted," I said. "Please don't be silly. I came here only because I'm wondering what has become of Corky and Joan. I haven't seen them since this morning, and I was getting worried."

Behind me Hacker grunted as he searched my person. And so, I thought, he *was* dangerously crazy! And my existence would soon be ended by a madman's bullet on a Mexican holiday. How the gods dally with us in the course of this absurd journey! My humble life as a schoolmaster, my aunts' fortune, Milo Murdoch's enmity, Joan's adulteries—what did they matter anyway? All would vanish in the squeezing of the trigger. Had Joan and I chosen another hotel, this would never have happened. A travel agent's recommendation had condemned me to death, and there was no use whining about the unfairness of it all. *Bad luck, old man* is what members of the English upper class say to these brutal encounters with Chance.

"Okay," said Hacker finally. "Turn around slowly and let's have a look at you. But no funny business or I'll drill ya. I'll shoot out your lights. I'll pump ya full of lead."

He turned on a lamp and ordered me to sit on one of

the beds. Standing over me he spread the fingers of his large hands. "As you can now plainly see," he said, "I have no revolver. That was merely a ruse. What was pointed at your spine was the large forefinger of my right hand. Hardened and polished from years of martial arts training. So you needn't bother trying to escape. If necessary I will apply force. And since I am much bigger than you, it follows that I will beat the daylights out of you. I'll thrash you within a square inch of your life. I'll knock you into next Sunday." He was bare-chested and wore only sockless tennis shoes and the striped Bermuda shorts. His hair was tousled and he was unshaven.

"I'm sorry, Ted," I said in a quiet voice. The insane, I had read somewhere, are often soothed by a calm, reasonable tone. It doesn't do to upset them by screaming. "I came quite innocently to your room in search of my wife. If I appear to have intruded, I certainly apologize. It was perhaps stupid of me to come in here like this. You probably suspected I was a burglar. Perfectly understandable."

Stepping back, he grasped a chair in both hands. With my eyes closed I waited for the furniture to come crashing down on my head. Instead, when I opened my eyes, I saw that Hacker had twisted the chair around, so that he now sat on it with his forearms resting across the back. He regarded me solemnly. "I await your explanation," he said.

"But I've already explained, Ted. I had been wondering about our wives. They've been gone all day."

"Our wives," he sneered, adding prissily, "and are you in the habit of walking into people's rooms unbidden?"

"Ted, you know perfectly well that I came here with no

intention other than to find my wife. And since she's obviously not here, I'll be on my way."

Hacker rose from his chair. "Make a move and you're a broken man," he said. "I'll chop you to pieces." He proceeded to slice the air with the edge of his hand. "The back of the neck," he cried. "Throat and kidneys, too. Your organs of increase. Nothing will be spared. At the end, you'll lie on the floor in a pitiful heap and beg for mercy."

"Ted, I beseech you."

Hacker sat down again. "Now, why don't you tell me the real reason why you're sneaking around my room at night?"

"But I've already told you!"

Great bursts of static interrupted the music from the radio and the light from the lamp fluttered. Hacker rested his chin on his forearms and studied me. "I knew you were working for them," he said. "Right from Day One I knew. Call it gut instinct. Another Fred Salisbury."

"Working for whom?" I asked. "I don't know what you're talking about."

"Ha, ha, ha, and again ha," said Hacker. "That's what they all say. *I don't know what you're talking about.* How many times in my long years of investigation have I heard that little declaration of innocence? An unanswerable question, of course, but I can assure you that if I had a penny, as they say."

"Just what are you talking about, Ted? I confess I'm baffled."

"Don't be cute, Philip. It doesn't sit right with me. I know you're working for them."

"Them?"

"You people think you've got the Caribbean all sewn up, don't you? Cuba. Nicaragua. El Salvador. Now Mexico. Taking advantage of the unstable conditions, the falling peso, etc. and etc. We're not stupid, Philip. We know your game. I watched you this afternoon from my balcony. I had the glasses on you and the chink. You two had quite a conversation by the pool."

"Are you referring to Mr. Yoshimodo?" I asked. "He's not Chinese, Ted, he's Japanese. He sells robots."

"Ha!" said Hacker. "The gentleman who took our pictures on the ferry sells robots. That's richly imagined."

"But he took the pictures with your camera, Ted. As a favour. Besides," I added, "all Japanese tourists take pictures."

"He was watching us by that historic ruin. It all fits."

"But what on earth do you imagine him to be? A Chinese Communist agent? That's ludicrous. The man is a respectable Japanese businessman. He's combining a little holiday with his business. He's been to Texas and now he's on his way home."

Hacker ran a hand through his hair. On the radio a señorita sang of love, I guess. Hacker looked exceedingly glum. "I've never trusted the nips either," he said. "You can't do business with them. They'll always give you the wet end of the stick. For years now Big has tried to talk turkey with Tokyo. But no dicey." He abruptly and outrageously broke wind. "Don't mind the dog, it won't bite," he said, staring past me. "They've come up with a suppository that's light years ahead of anything we've developed. They're killing us in the big cities." He shook his head. "I don't know whether to believe you or not, Phil. You remind me an awful lot of Fred Salisbury. If there's something fishy going on between you and the Oriental, I want to hear about it."

"Ted, I swear."

Hacker got up quickly and, walking to the window, looked past the billowing curtains at the black night. Thunder rumbled away in the distance. "I guess my nerves are bad, Phil," he said, turning and walking back toward me. "Business hasn't been all that hot lately. I thought this little vacation might help." He looked down at me. "How are your nerves, by the way?"

"Not too good at times, Ted."

He sighed. "I thought as much. It's the dreadful times in which we live, Phil. A period of chaos and moral confusion. Can I offer you some refreshment? A drink? A tranquilizing powder? Come along!" He seized my arm. "Let us see what we can find to ease our troubled minds." Holding my arm he led me to the bathroom where he switched on the light.

In the stark yellow room he looked palely angry. A small clothesline had been strung across the shower stall, and it was filled with Corky Hacker's underclothes. "Look at this place!" cried Hacker. "You would think she would show some consideration, wouldn't you? I mean, suppose *I* wanted to take a shower? Would I not have to remove all these step-ins and brassieres and pantyhose and whatnot? Why should I have to do that? No consideration at all."

Hacker released my arm and, bending down, began to rummage in an athletic bag under the sink. "It's the little things that get you down in the end," he said. "The toenails left on the edge of the bathtub. The missing cap from the tube of toothpaste. The hair *clogging* the drain!" He stood up holding a vinyl case. "Have you ever seen Big's Travel-Pal, Phil?"

"No."

The stubble on his face was touched lightly with grey. "This," he said, weighing the vinyl case in his hand, "is a very popular item with the more affluent members of the travelling public. Executives and ministers of state and people of that ilk. You will often find these in the luggage of first-class passengers."

Hacker unzippered the case. Inside were several little jars and vials and tubes. "There is," said Hacker, "everything here for the hard-pressed person of affairs." His long forefinger pointed at several items. "The usual nostrums for the relief of headache, lumbago, and nervous fits. Corn plasters for the weary and the footsore. A pink solution for cramps, diarrhea, and general tummy turbulence. A prune extract pummelled into powdered form for pokey peristalsis. I am, of course, quoting from the company's literature." Like a merchant displaying a rare jewel, he pointed to a tiny vial. "Amyl nitrite. A great favourite with people in the motion-picture industry. It's supposed to prolong the rapture of the one-night stand. And over here we have diazepam in two-, five-, and ten-milly sizes. There are even a couple of twenties for those travelling to other hemispheres who want a real man's sleep. But I don't recommend the twenties, Phil. We market those mostly to the Rubber Room Lodges. One of those babies will put a big fat axe killer to sleep in no time at all. But say, listen, I don't take any of this crap myself. When I want to relax, I like a good smoke. What was it Kipling said—'A woman is only a woman, but a good cigar is a smoke.'"

In a little compartment of the Travel-Pal lay several neatly stacked cigarettes. "Do you use hemp, Phil?" asked Hacker.

"No, never," I said.

"Doesn't hurt once in a while. No more than a large Scotch."

"I couldn't," I said. "I've spoken against the use of drugs in chapel."

"Have you really?"

"Yes."

"Well, this will just make you a hypocrite. But so what? Let him who is without sin cast the first stone. Light up, pal."

"I don't think so, Ted."

"Take one, Phil. Immediately." His gaunt face looked pained. I fingered one of the marijuana cigarettes. A lighter magically appeared in Hacker's hand and a three-inch flame blazed. "We deserve it, Phil," he said. "All year we work our fingers to the bone. Now we'll have a little holiday with the hemp. What's the harm?" He put the flame under my cigarette. "Heave her back, pal, and wait for the fog to clear. Runway Twenty-nine looks pretty good. We'll be airborne in minutes."

I coughed miserably.

"Steady as she goes," said Hacker, slapping my back. "You'll get used to it. Meantime, let us retire to the main part of these gruesome lodgings."

This we did, and I sat on the bed staring at a cane-bottomed chair. Hacker opened the door of his small refrigerator. "Let's have some cold beer with this," he said. "A little hemp and cold beer go down very nicely together." He handed me a can of Carta Blanca.

"I wonder," I said, "what happened to our wives?"

"Who cares?" said Hacker.

On the radio two men with guitars sang of love, I suppose. But then I heard women's voices coming along the balcony. I listened to Joan's braying laughter. "The girls are back," I cried.

Hacker again sat in the chair with his arms hanging over the back.

"This better be good," he muttered.

Twenty-One

They switched on the overhead light and entered the room. Corky Hacker had changed her costume; she now wore a tight-fitting black cocktail dress and strapless high-heel shoes. Joan was still in her pants and shirt. Both women had bought large straw coolie hats and these were on their heads. "Greetings, gents," said Joan. "What's the poop?"

Corky Hacker laid several parcels on the bed beside me. "I smell something naughty but nice. Why, I do believe the boys are into the weed," she cried.

Joan stood over me, arms akimbo. "Philip Bannister," she mocked. "Shame on you! A respectable schoolmaster!" I looked up at her, feeling pleasantly light-headed.

Hacker continued to stare grimly at the two women. Corky went over and, standing behind her husband, began to knead his shoulder muscles. "And how is my Teddykins?" she asked, nuzzling his neck. Her straw hat fell off and wobbled into a corner. I watched its brief journey with a feeling of almost unbearable sadness.

"What did my big bear do all day?" asked Corky.

"What did *you* do all day is perhaps more to the point?" said Hacker. "And where did you get that slinky-looking thing. I don't remember you packing that. Do you realize it's nearly eleven o'clock? You and your friend here have been gone for over twelve hours. I demand an explanation."

Corky Hacker stepped around to face her husband. Leaning forward, she rested her hands on her knees and brought her face to within inches of Hacker's. "Is my bear in a bad mood?" Looking over at my wife she said, "What are we going to do with these two characters, Joan?"

"Well, I, for one, am going to have a drink," Joan said.

"You better watch it. The statistics on dipsomania among modern women are frightening."

"Oh piffle!" said Joan.

"Keep a civil tongue in your head," I cried.

"Felicitously phrased, Phil," said Hacker.

Joan shrugged and walked to the dresser. "I'll just have tonic water, Joan," said Corky, looking at her husband.

"Well!" said Hacker.

Corky sat on the other bed. "Well, we just had a fun day that's all. This morning we went on one of those glass bottom boats. Gosh, Teddy, the fish! Some of them are so cute."

"Yes yes, the cute fish. Go on."

"Then after lunch we shopped and just walked around the village until the shops closed for the siesta. Then we took a taxi to one of the big luxury hotels south of the village. We went for a swim in their pool. No one even bothered to ask if we were guests. Then we went to their bar for a couple of drinks. And then we had dinner."

"Did you meet any men?"

"Oh, gosh no, Teddy. You know I wouldn't."

"I know nothing of the sort," said Hacker. "And I'll bet you spent a lot of money shopping, too."

"Not really. I just bought a couple of dresses and a coral necklace. Some T-shirts. I got Mom and Dad Hacker a nice plate. Native craftsmanship. Do you want to see it?"

Hacker made an extremely ugly face suggesting pain. "A plate!" He stuck out his tongue.

"It's really lovely."

"They've got a lot of plates," said Hacker grumpily. "What are they going to do with another plate, for crying out loud? It's a dumb idea."

"It's only a souvenir. A little momentum of our holidays."

"You mean memento, you dumb bitch."

Corky Hacker's eyes filled with tears. "You're being horrid to me, Teddy."

Hacker observed her with calm dislike. "Oh, go ahead and cry. Boo hoo hoo all you like. A fat lot I care."

"How is your drink, sweetheart?" asked Joan.

"More beer," I ordered. My throat felt parched. Joan brought me a can of beer and, sitting down beside me, nibbled my left ear, which had suddenly begun to ring. Like the clock tower in Bung Hall, it pleasantly chimed the quarter hours, and soon my right ear followed by striking the hours to eleven. To Joan's amusement I counted each stroke of the clapper.

"I'm glad you're not the jealous type, darling," whispered Joan.

The sound of the bells ceased. "Who says I'm not?"

"Ted's so insecure, isn't he? It's all so silly."

"Stop that whispering," Hacker shouted. "I won't be whispered about."

"And quite right too, Ted," I said.

Hacker drained his can of beer. "Let's have another beer, woman!" His wife smiled nervously and went to the little refrigerator.

"What about you, Phil?" asked Hacker. "More hemp?"

"Might as well be hung for a sheep as a lamb."

"You're damn right. That's the kind of language I want to hear." I watched him move toward the bathroom. Without a doubt it was the drug, but Hacker's tennis shoes did not appear to be touching the floor. I marvelled at his progress through the air. My wife also floated to another part of the room.

Hacker returned with two more marijuana cigarettes. The bed sagged as he sat beside me. Putting his arm around my shoulder he said, "Forget about that earlier stuff, Phil. I didn't mean anything by it. I was just kidding you. See, ever since I've been a little kid I've always wanted to talk the way they do in the movies. But who ever gets a chance in real life? It was just the harmless little fantasy of an ordinary mortal." He chuckled. "I guess I gave you quite a scare, didn't I?"

"Yes, you did, Ted," I said. "I only wish I'd had a poker. Or perhaps an eight-pound maul. You'd have danced to a different tune then, I'll wager."

"Now don't be heartless, Phil."

• • •

Joan watched us from across the room. "I thought whispering was forbidden in this room," she said. "What are you chaps up to, anyway?"

"None of your beeswax," said Hacker.

I inhaled more hot smoke.

"You're always butting in where you're not wanted," said Hacker. "If I was your husband, I'd give you a knuckle sandwich for supper."

"Do tell!" laughed Joan, sticking out her tailored behind. "How about some paddywhacks for starters?"

Corky Hacker covered her mouth with a hand and giggled.

Hacker stared at Joan's considerable backside. "Women!" He sounded disgusted. "That's all they ever think about, isn't it? They never get enough. Wear a fellow out. They seem to think all we have to do after a hard day's work is get the old ready roger. I mean that the other way around, of course. What was it Sophocles said about sex?"

"I don't recall," I said. I was calmly awaiting the quarter hour.

"Was he queer?" asked Hacker. "Or was that Socrates?"

"Let's have a party," said Joan. "For goodness sakes, we're on holidays. Next week we'll be back at the old grinderoo." She turned up the radio and some rock music with a Latin beat began to punish the air.

Straightening her straw hat, Joan started to dance. Corky soon moved in beside her, while Hacker and I watched them in gloomy silence. After a moment he said, "Do you know something, Phil?"

"What?"

"I have of late, but wherefore I know not, lost all my mirth."

"Foregone all custom of exercises," I continued, "and indeed it goes so heavily with my disposition that this goodly frame, the earth, seems to me a sterile promontory."

Hacker hugged me tightly. "It's so good to have a buddy." The dancing women moved near us. "Observe," said Hacker, "the lewd wenches! How they seek to tempt us!"

In the scented air Corky Hacker floated in front of us. "Come on, you big bear, and get your honey!"

"My Cork is a wanton hussy," said Hacker, and at once buried his head in her midriff.

I arose and advanced toward my wife, who smiled at me. As we circled one another, she undid the necktie and cast aside the coolie hat. Sitting on the edge of the bed, Hacker had somehow contrived to work his head beneath his wife's tight dress. He was there busily engaged, and it was a very odd sight indeed. Joan noticed too and, stirred by this connubial tableau, thrust her groin toward me. Snapping my fingers above my head, I executed a perfect pirouette.

I am not without a basic sense of rhythm, and one lonely summer long ago took tango lessons from Miss Ida Courtney of the Nu-Dance School. I was, I think, her only pupil. In an empty hall over the offices of a driving academy, Miss Courtney praised my footwork, and on a final August afternoon, kissed my hot cheek and left me desolated. And so in the El Gringo Hotel on that black Wednesday night, I manoeuvred smartly around my wife. Across the room Corky Hacker, with eyes closed, swayed over the great head beneath her dress and moaned softly. She was in, I suppose, some initial state of sexual delirium. I concluded that my first orgy was about to begin, and both my ears chimed merrily.

Twenty-Two

When Joan arose from the cane-bottomed chair, I discovered that her naked rump had been scored by the chair's design. Imprinted on the dimpled flesh was an empty crossword puzzle whose squares awaited the letters that convey the secrets of everlasting felicity. Studying those small blank spaces gave me truthfully as much pleasure as I have ever had in my life. Joan stood to recite from Lord Tennyson's "In Memoriam."

> Unwatch'd the garden bough shall sway
> The tender blossoms flutter down

A favourite selection of mine, and as I listened to the solemn beauty of the words, I continued to ponder the magnificent cryptogram before me. At some vanished moment, we had removed all our clothes and, briefly, I grew anxious over the fate of my polka-dot boxer shorts. The purple dots on their white background assumed a sudden and vast importance; I was prepared to grieve over their loss. Then, like a man awakening to finger bandages, I placed my hand above my right ear and realized that I was indeed wearing them on my head. I lack the gifts to express the happiness afforded me by this discovery.

After Joan finished, Hacker hurried across the room to

congratulate her. I, too, stood up and shook hands with my wife. I suggested the four of us should try to arrange an annual holiday together.

"What a jolly good idea!" said Joan, kissing my cheek.

"You're all right, Phil," said Hacker. "In fact, you're better than all right. You're aces." We shook hands. "I'll tell you the God's honest, though. At first, I thought you were just a stuffy, uptight little Canadian shit. But I was wrong. Absolutely dead wrong. You're a scholar and a gentleman. I can see that now, and I hereby apologize for my previous wrong-headed impression."

"No need to apologize," I said. "And may I add, Ted, that I, too, was guilty of a serious error in judgment. At first I took you for just another vulgar, loud-mouthed, know-it-all American. Some kind of ape, in fact."

"These surface impressions," said Hacker grandly. "How they perpetuate cultural stereotypes!"

"Now I can see that you're just a fun-loving guy. Easy-going and at home with his fellow creatures."

"I can," said Hacker, "be a lot of laughs, that's true."

"You're all right, Ted."

"Thanks, pal. In a moment I'm going to fuck your wife. I hope you don't mind."

"Not at all. Please help yourself."

"Let me shake your hand again, Fred."

"Phil."

"Of course, Phil."

We again shook hands, and Joan put her arms around the both of us. "You two sweet chaps!"

"I would just like to say, Joan," I said, "that upon our return home I had planned to divorce you."

"What a droll idea!"

"Now I'm not so sure. You recited that Tennyson beautifully."

"Thank you, my pet."

"I love Tennyson. You did him proud."

"Thank you again, dear boy."

"And where, pray, is that splendid wife of yours, Ted? Is she still in the bathroom? By George, if she's still in the tub, I intend to join her forthwith." I laughed very loudly. "Join her! I think that's rather good. I would venture to say that the Monkey Trick is not entirely out of the question. I shall, of course, require instructions."

"Oh, she's not in the tub, pal," said Hacker. "She's putting on her outfit. She promised me a treat. In fact, I had best see to the music. As your dear helpmate would say, I shan't be a trice."

He went to a small table and began sorting through a stack of tape cassettes, peering at each one under the lampshade. Looking at him I thought he was a fine figure of a man. I smiled at my wife. "Isn't it amazing how uninhibited one feels when one is travelling."

"Indeed one does and indeed it is!" said Joan.

"Who would have thought it!" I exclaimed. Joan was looking at Hacker while I noted that the squares on her buttocks were fading. Soon they would be gone forever! I experienced a brief but powerful sense of loss. A rush of feeling. A heart pang over what may never be again.

Bent across his machine, Hacker called out, "Are you ready, Cork?"

"Yes, Teddy," she cried from the bathroom.

Hacker punched various buttons, and the room was filled with the music of a marching band. It was a Sousa tune, and it sounded cheerfully incongruous in the black

Mexican night. Hacker stood listening thoughtfully by his machine. I, too, was stirred by the music, remembering October Saturdays when the Gannymede varsity lined up to kick off to the hated Bollocks Hall Bulldogs. Along the sidelines, old Gannymedians wearing animal skins and fur coats drank whiskey from flasks.

From the bathroom Corky Hacker emerged wearing a majorette costume of crimson and silver. Her breathtaking legs were encased in high boots. Smiling, she began to prance to the music. We gasped as she threw her baton in the air. It grazed the ceiling, but as it fell she caught it and handled it with a wonderful dexterity. When she reached her husband, Corky Hacker stopped and, marking time, placed one hand on her hip, and with the other hand twirled the coloured stick above her head. It spun like the blades of a tiny helicopter. When she turned to strut again across the room, Hacker fell in behind her and, swinging his long arms, kept in perfect step. On their next pass Joan and I left the reviewing stand and joined them, so that we all four marched to the end of the rousing tune. When it was over, Hacker, panting a little, turned off the cassette and gazed fondly at his wife.

"That was great, Cork!"

"Thank you, Teddy," said Corky Hacker, shyly looking down at her great tasselled boots.

"It certainly was," I said. "An inspired performance."

"A jolly good show!" said Joan.

Hacker had a sickly grin on his face. "You sure you don't mind, kiddo?" he said to me.

I put my arm around Corky Hacker's waist. "Not at all, Ted."

"Shall we play in your court or mine?" asked Hacker.

"It gets damn cold at nights down here, doesn't it?" said Joan, pulling a blanket off the bed and draping it over her shoulders.

"It does get chilly," I said, removing the polka-dot boxer shorts from my head and climbing into them. Hacker commenced to stuff handfuls of himself into a pair of Jockey shorts.

"Let's not," said Joan, "be boringly bourgeois about all this. There's surely room enough for all right here in this very room. Why don't Ted and I take that bed," she said, pointing, "and Ted, your wife and my husband can commit adultery over here."

"Oh!" cried Corky Hacker, "you make it all sound so *dirty*."

"But it's going to be dirty, my dear," said Joan. "At least, I jolly well hope so."

Corky Hacker's cheeks were splashed with tears. "Oh, it shouldn't be dirty," she said. "Sex should be beautiful. It's the most beautiful event in the world."

She began to cry and Hacker put his arm around her. "Now come on, honey bunny, don't be like that. You've got to be a good sport."

Corky hid her face in his shoulder. "I don't want to be a good sport."

"Well, that tears it," said Joan, and, pulling the blanket tightly about her, she padded barefoot across the room in search of cigarettes. She looked like some old Inca priestess.

"Oh, the Cork will be all right," said Hacker, patting his wife's back. "Now listen," he whispered, "your big bear wuves you. You know that. This is just a little fun. Remember the party at Fred Salisbury's? No harm done."

Corky Hacker cried piteously. "Oh, I hated that man!" She suddenly broke away from her husband and walked swiftly to the balcony.

Hacker shrugged and stroked his heavy jaw. "What do you say we turn off the lights? It's always more fun in the dark."

"Do you really think so?" said Joan. She was now sitting cross-legged on the bed puffing on a Parliament. "I've always fancied a gander myself. Philip and I always leave the lights on, don't we, my jewel?"

"Come to think of it," I said, "I suppose we do. Never thought much about it, to tell you the truth."

Hacker gave me an unfriendly look. "And I suppose you've got a mirror over your bed, too?" Joan snorted. "The Salisburys had a mirror," said Hacker, looking toward the balcony where his wife was leaning against the railing. "Look folks," he said, "I'm sorry about this. It's just that Corky's a little modest. You have to understand that she's just a small-town girl."

"Don't worry about it," I said. We were now whispering. "Perhaps I'm not her type."

"Well, that could be, of course," said Hacker.

"Well, what's wrong with just the three of us having some fun?" said Joan. Hacker winced. He didn't seem to think much of the idea, and truth to tell neither did I.

"Why don't you go out and have a word with her?" said Hacker. "Give her a little pitch. You never know."

"It seems a bit unfair," I said. "I mean, the two of you in here. While we're out there. *Talking*."

Hacker laughed dryly. "Oh, *life* is unfair, old man. Haven't you noticed that yet? Now listen. Go and talk to the girl. I'm sure she'll come around."

Joan stubbed out her cigarette. "Well, let's get the show on the road or I'm going to have a snooze. We did a lot of running around today." She yawned hugely.

On the balcony Corky Hacker stood with her arms folded across her chest. The wind had dried her tears and raised gooseflesh on her bare legs. I leaned on the railing beside her and we both stared grimly at the palm trees and the dark sea and directly below us the green lighted water of the swimming pool. "That was a wonderful performance," I said. "It must have taken a great deal of practice to acquire those skills."

"Oh, don't bother patronizing me, Philip," she said.

"But I wasn't . . ."

"But for your information I once performed before sixty thousand people in Texas Stadium. I placed ninth out of three hundred girls from all over America."

"That's quite an achievement."

"It was won that year by Mary Jean Beiderhoff of Arlo, Texas. Do you know who Mary Jean Beiderhoff is today?" Her voice trembled with indignation.

"No."

"Why, she's Eleanor Petty in 'Storm of Life.' I see her every fucking day on television. And," added Corky bitterly, "if I had scored just *three* points higher, I might have beaten her. And maybe now *I* would be Eleanor Petty."

The palm fronds rattled in the wind and from somewhere below us came the sound of singing voices. I strained to listen. *Happy birthdaaaaaaay, dear Freddy. Happy birthday to you!*

"Everyone thinks I'm just a dumb little broad," said Corky.

"Not at all."

"I just do that dopey routine because Ted gets a kick out of it."

"I see."

"Ted's pretty weird, isn't he?"

"He's an unusual man, certainly."

"But the thing is, I love him, see!"

Corky Hacker hugged her arms, and I thought of the little stone cell at Tulum. "Even though he's loud and ignorant, I'm crazy about the guy. And he has no friends. No one at the Okey-Dokey Club likes him. We hardly ever go there anymore because people can't stand Ted's jokes. He used to buy those buzzers that give people shocks when you shake hands with them. Or he'd have a flower in his lapel that squirted water in your face. Or one of those whoopee cushions that make rude sounds when you sit on them. Stuff like that. People just got tired of it. They'd see him coming and run the other way. But if I left him, he'd crack up. Why, he'd go to pieces just like that!" She startled me by snapping her fingers before my eyes.

"He's certainly lucky to have you," I said, glancing behind me.

I saw Hacker bent across his tape machine punching buttons. He still wore his Jockey shorts. The device poured forth some trashy dance music. I turned from the wind and with difficulty lighted the remains of my second marijuana cigarette.

"Oh, can I have some?" asked Corky. "Teddy and I smoke a lot of grass together. Of course, it's better if you do it indoors. Out here we're so . . . so *ventilated*!" She laughed and took an enormous lungful of smoke, holding it for what seemed like minutes. As she exhaled, her eyes crossed slightly. I puffed and coughed and was rewarded by a faint peal of bells.

Hacker and Joan were now beneath the covers and from under the moving bundle of bedclothes came laughter and the sounds of sexual commotion. I said, "I wonder what they're doing in there. Or, perhaps more to the point, how?"

Leaning on the railing, Corky Hacker sank a fist into her cheek. "Love is so mysterious, isn't it?"

"Yes, I suppose so," I replied, rubbing my scorched lips and flinging the cigarette into the wind. We watched the sparks scattering in the dark.

"I'm going to write a novel about love someday," said Corky. "Remember I told you about that creative-writing course I took at the university? And the story about Polly?"

"Yes. I remember Polly and her gas meter man."

"Well, I might use some of that in the novel, though mostly it's going to be about me." She leaned over and scratched her knee. "I think I'll start it this summer when Ted goes fishing up in Minnesota with Dad Hacker. They go for a month every summer. They've done it since Ted was eight or nine years old. It's a father-and-son thing, and so I'm left for the whole of August. So maybe that's when I'll start."

She stared dreamily out at the night. "Maybe it'll become a best seller. I'm going to put in all about growing up in my hometown. And then being selected Cheer Queen. And then the Tri-State Finals. Then Texas Stadium and all those people cheering. Also how I met Ted. But I'll change a lot, too. I'll make up things. I'll invent several lovers." She laughed. "People like lots of screwing in their novels. I even have a title. I'm going to call it *Love in the Wind*."

Behind us I could hear Hacker and Joan thrashing about. My wife's donkey laughter had evolved into a kind of whinny.

"Do you like it?" asked Corky.

"What?"

"My title, *Love in the Wind*. Do you like it?"

"I suppose so. What does it mean?"

"Oh, it doesn't mean anything," she said. "It just sounds mysterious. I read somewhere that *wind* is one of the most popular words in a book title."

"Is that so?"

"*Love*, of course, is a favourite, too," said Corky Hacker. "Especially with women. Gee, you look cute in those shorts, Philip. Let's dance."

Your Excellency, Your Worthiness, Your Radiance (I must ask Mr. Gomez how to address the bench in this country), we danced on the balcony of the El Gringo Hotel to a thousand and one violins. Corky Hacker shivered in the wind and pressed her treacherous bare legs against my flying frontispiece. Her breath was warm on my face, and from the tape machine a crooner crooned of love, I think. Beyond my partner's fragrant hair, I glimpsed one of Joan's legs as it emerged from under the covers.

"You're a terrific dancer, Philip."

"Thank you, my dear," I said, watching my wife's long alabaster limb curl over the mound of bedding I took to be the Nebraskan's back.

"I just love dancing," said Corky. "I remember our prom as if it were yesterday. I'm going to make it a big scene in my novel because it was my first date with Ted. He looked so handsome in his tuxedo. I wore a pale blue evening dress. The orchestra played 'The Way We Were.' I couldn't help it. I cried."

I listened with a happy heart as my right ear faintly knelled the hours to midnight. "Will you do me a favour?" I asked.

"Uh huh," said the sleepy little voice across my shoulder.

"Will you take off your costume and sit on the cane-bottomed chair for five minutes?"

Corky stepped back to clap a hand across her mouth. Then she pushed me gently on the chest and laughed. "You quiet guys always want the weird stuff, don't you?"

From the room came a cry that was sudden and terrible. A vocable to dissolve the bowels of mortal men. Alarmed (was it pain or ecstasy?), we peered through the open balcony door and beheld the bedclothes rising like an act of sorcery. A moment later Ted Hacker tumbled onto the floor where he lay moaning as he kneaded one of his legs.

"It's his calf again," explained Corky, sprinting toward the bathroom in her great boots. "I'll get the Heet, Teddy," she called.

In his violent descent, Hacker had stripped the bed of all coverings, so that, like some character in a French farce, Joan now sat up revealed and astonished. "Well, I'll be damned," she said, lighting a Parliament. On the floor, Hacker, still wearing his shorts, writhed in agony. Corky returned with the liniment and applied it to the afflicted part. Leaning back on his elbows, Hacker sighed with relief.

"My poor bear," Corky murmured. "Is it feeling any better?"

"A little." Hacker sounded mournful. "Darn charley horse."

"He gets it every so often," said Corky, looking first at Joan and then at me.

"It's been months now," said Hacker. "The last time was just before Christmas. Just as I was getting off the plane in Minneapolis. All that sitting I suppose. It just cramped up on me."

Joan exhaled smoke noisily from the bed while I sat in the cane-bottomed chair and debated with myself the question of whether to remove my underpants. Was it possible, I wondered, to stand with my back to the bathroom mirror and, looking over my shoulder, study my own design?

Twenty-Three

"I can't believe we go home the day after tomorrow," said Joan. "Why, it hardly seems possible for a week to have gone by so quickly."

"It's been a fun few days, all right," said Hacker, yawning. "There's no doubt about that."

"And none of us has even been sick," said Corky. "Aren't you supposed to get sick in Mexico?"

"A touch of the collywobbles," Hacker said, pouring beer from a can down his gullet. "To be expected in tropical climes."

We were speeding through the darkness of early morning in the Volkswagen buggy. The empty pale highway stretched before us like a ribbon through the jungle. We had already passed the hotel area and were several miles beyond the village. We were on our way to the other side of the island to greet the sunrise. A few hours before, this excursion had sounded like the last word in good ideas. Now it seemed only foolish, though no one had come forth to say as much. In point of fact, an edginess had overtaken one and all; we had been in each other's company too long and we had not slept much. The evening itself had not even approached dissoluteness. Following Hacker's summary collapse as lover, we had smoked more marijuana and drunk more beer, the Hackers reclining on the floor with the soles of their bare feet touching. In this manner they may have been transmitting and receiving sexual messages, for they lay smiling while I read the entire one hundred and fifty-two pages of *Let's Discover Mexico!* by Matilda L. Farp. Meanwhile Joan dozed, abruptly awakened from time to time by her own monstrous snorting sounds.

It was in the Farp book that I read of the old Mayan custom of observing the sunrise; in days gone by, Cozumel was a holy place, visited by pilgrims from the mainland. Watching the eastern sky at daybreak was supposed to ensure good health for the coming year. With this in mind we had set out, and in the little open car sat in grumpy silence, speeding along the coastal road toward a benediction from the gods who, ever playfully ironic, had granted to the Hackers and to Joan but one more hour of life.

Hacker finished his beer and, crumpling the can in his fist, hurled the container into the underbrush.

"Teddy, you shouldn't litter," said Corky, who was seated alongside Joan in the back.

"Aw nuts!" said Hacker.

"Americans always get blamed for littering," Corky said in a voice charged with resentment. "Why don't they blame Norwegians or Chinamen? I'll bet they litter just as much as we do."

On the jungle side of the highway, the birds were starting to twitter and gabble. On the other side, the ocean went about its ancient business, though the wind had dropped and the waves broke gently over the gnarled clumps of coral. Daylight was beginning to seep into the sky.

Numbed by sleeplessness, we drove in silence for several minutes until Hacker cried aloud, "Oh, for goodness sakes, can't somebody sing or whistle or something? This is more like a funeral than a party." Taking his own suggestion he began to sing in a voice that crackled with irritation, "Boola boolah, boola boolah . . . boola boola boola boola boola boo. Come on everybody! Sing!"

"Is that an order?" I asked.

"Don't be funny, Phil."

"Well, I, for one, refuse to sing such nonsense."

Hacker gave me a sidelong glance and then returned his attention to the road. "So you think it's nonsense, do you?"

"Yes. It most assuredly is nonsense."

"And you're too good for nonsense, are you, you pompous little poop."

"Pompous or not, it remains nonsense and my lips are sealed."

The tires hummed along the pavement. Behind me Joan had dropped into sleep and was snoring. Hacker finally said, "You sang that goofy school song. Before we played Ruthless Landlord. Remember? That was nonsense."

"I was tight. You have to make allowances."

"Allowances!" said Hacker. "Ha!"

"Teddy," cried Corky, "you're driving too fast."

"Oh shut up," said Hacker, clearing his throat. "I am now going to sing 'The Nebraska Fight Song.' " Amazed and fearful birds flew from the treetops and, surfacing to consciousness, Joan mumbled what, what, and what again. Corky Hacker joined her husband in the singing of the chorus.

When they finished, there was a terrible moment of silence. The very air was filled with hostility and rage. Then in a light pleasant voice Corky sang "Climb Every Mountain." At the end, her voice faltered. "I'm sorry, guys, but that song always gets me where I live."

Hacker, too, had been strongly affected by the song and cleared his throat again. "No need to apologize, hon. That was just great."

Joan made several smacking noises with her lips betokening wakefulness. "I suppose I can put my oar in," she said.

"Good girl, Joanie," said Hacker.

Joan started in on "Waltzing Matilda" and the Hackers sang along on the chorus. At the end of that performance, Hacker looked over at me. "Your turn, Phil," he said quietly. I told him I would sing "The Teddy Bears' Picnic," and Hacker made a strangled noise in his throat. "'The Teddy Bears' Picnic'? For the love of Mike, are you serious?"

"Perfectly," I said. "It's a favourite of mine." Turning to Hacker's staring eyes I sang,

If you go down to the woods today
You'd better not go alone.

The song revived a pleasant memory of nursery days. I stood singing next to my Aunt Flo who was seated at the piano; in a chair nearby, Aunty Fay struck a tin drum with tiny wooden sticks.

When I had finished, Hacker shook his head and, pulling off to the side of the road, stopped the vehicle. In the grey light we watched seabirds passing over the water.

Hacker opened another can of beer. "Well," he said, frowning, "here we are! What do we do now?"

"We wait for the sun to rise," I said. "Then we throw ourselves upon the beach. We prostrate ourselves and ask for the sun god's blessing."

"Are you crazy?" said Hacker, looking at me. "Prostrate ourselves?"

"I think Philip is pulling your leg, Teddy," said Corky.

"Oh yeah," said Hacker. "Well, I can pull a few legs, too, if the need arises. As well as wring a few necks if it comes to that." He gulped some beer and squeezed the can between thumb and forefinger.

"For corn's sakes. Sunrises and 'The Teddy Bears' Picnic.' Next thing we'll be reciting more poetry."

"May I remind you, Ted," said Joan indignantly, "that my dear late husband was a poet of very considerable distinction in his own land. And I will not have you ridiculing his life's work, and the work of other literary artists."

"Hear, hear," I said.

"Oh, do shut up, Philip," said Joan. "You're ever so eager to insert your tuppence worth of sarcasm."

"But I wasn't being sarcastic, my pet. I agree with your sentiments. Literature must be defended against the barbarians."

"Are you calling me a barbarian, you little twerp?" said Hacker.

"Not," I continued, "that I think your late husband wrote anything that could remotely be called literature. Still, hats off for effort. Poor old Tushy tried. He was in there bowling."

"Bowling?" said Joan. "What in the name of goodness are you talking about? Bowling?"

"It's from the noble game of cricket. You should know that, Joan. Australia has produced some fine cricketers in her day."

"You are becoming a source of some concern to me,

Philip. I shouldn't wonder if that marijuana hasn't damaged your brain cells."

"Very likely," said Hacker.

"I think we've all had too much to smoke and drink," Corky said. She shivered. "It sure gets chilly in the early morning, doesn't it?"

Joan said, "It's damn close to freezing, I should imagine."

"I should imagine," I murmured.

"Are you mocking me, you insolent man?" asked Joan.

Hacker wagged his head from side to side and turned to the women. "He's very good at mocking people, isn't he? He's also very good at calling people names."

"Why don't we play a game while we're waiting for the sun to come up?" asked Corky.

Hacker groaned. "What kind of game?"

"How about I Spy," I said. "As a child I played I Spy with my aunts."

"His *aunts*!" said Hacker. "He played with his *aunts*, for mercy's sake."

"You're damn right. And great sports they were, too."

"How about Hide-and-Go-Seek?" asked Corky.

"We played that, too," I said.

"Hide-and-Go-Seek," said Joan. "It sounds just bizarre enough to be fun. Besides, it'll get us off our bums. Warm us up."

"An excellent point," I said, turning to smile at Joan, who glowered at me. She looked about ready to box my ears.

Corky reached over and, grasping her husband's earlobes, began to pull them, singing gently,

This is the way we milk the cow
Milk the cow, milk the cow
This is the way we milk the cow
Early in the morning.

"What about it, hon?" she asked. "Hide-and-Go-Seek?"

Hacker shrugged. "Oh, all right." He jerked a thumb toward me. "But he's *it*. The three of us will hide. You have to close your eyes and count to seventy-five, Bannister. And no peeking! The Volkswagen is home."

"Agreed," I said.

Of course, I did not close my eyes; I expect very few people do. Through splayed fingers I watched them disappear along an abandoned road into the gloom of the jungle. Out to sea the sky was brightening and the horizon lay open like a wound. It was going to be a hot day.

As I walked along the overgrown road, the birds shrieked and flew from branches. With the possibility of encountering a large snake in mind, I began to sing a jaunty version of "The Teddy Bears' Picnic," remembering how my aunts would seek me out from dark corners of the house on Sparrow Hill Road. I could see Aunty Flo opening the door to a storage room on the third floor, where, behind a horsehair sofa piled high with books and boxes, I crouched in gleeful fear. And listened paralytic in damp underpants to her breathy imitation of Mary Jordan, a local axe murderess, famous for beheading all six of her children. "Now, where's Master Bannister," whispered my aunt. "I very much suspect he's about. Why, my axe can hear his heartbeat and is hungry for a lean young neck."

From the underbrush came a terrifying squeal that quickened my heart. I pictured some tiny luckless creature surviving the night, only to fall at dawn into the jaws of an enemy. The sound unnerved me, and, standing on that disused road among the palmetto and ferns, I was seized by a spectacular anxiety. Looking back I can now see that it was probably a confluence of circumstances: the terrible strangeness of the landscape, and my own drugged fatigue distorting and corrupting my imagination. Yet standing under the awakening sky I felt utterly estranged. It was as though I were the last person on earth. There was no sign of the others, and I spoke aloud to the shadowy trees. "Now, where oh where can these people be, I wonder? The belle of the Southern Hemisphere and my bride! And the nice couple from the breadbasket of America!"

The birds chattered back at me as I sang, "Come out, come out, wherever you are! And see the nice lady who fell from a star. You will remember *The Wizard of Oz*. Dorothy has just landed in Munchkin Land . . ." The forest swallowed my words. A small bird cocked his head to regard me. "Well," I shouted. "I'm going back now, *mes amis*." I paused and listened. "It'll soon be sunup, podners. We'll miss the risin'. There's flapjacks and eggs and hot coffee in the chuckwagon."

He must have been hiding behind a tree. I had no chance as he struck from behind. His arm encircled my throat and my knees buckled.

"Gaaaah, Hacker," I croaked as I clawed at his arm. We sank to our knees and lay hunched over the road, looking perhaps like two enormous amphibians at intercourse.

Hacker's breath was in my ear. "I never did like you very much, Bannister, you little twit."

"Gaaaah!"

"You think you're pretty hot stuff, don't you?"

"Gaaaah!"

"I'll bet you can't even get it up."

I nodded my head to deny this. "You're lucky that cramp hit me," he said. "Or everafter your wife would have laughed you to scorn."

"A lame excuse," I gasped.

Hacker thumped me hard on the back. "Oh, get up, you little fart. Come on!" He stood over me, while on hands and knees I continued to gaze at the grass by the side of the road. In fact, I was looking for a large stick to use on my assailant. "Come on, Phil, get up," said Hacker. "I didn't mean to hurt you. Sometimes I just get fed up. And maybe I don't know my own strength. I'm very strong, aren't I? Are you going to be all right? I just felt like trying a little manoeuvre we learned in the marines."

I stood up and fingered my bruised throat. A headache had invaded my right temple. Hacker stuck his thumbs in the rear pockets of his jeans and looked up the road. "The girls are just up ahead. They sent me back to get you. There's something real interesting up there. An old airfield. We'll have a look. It's better than playing Hide-and-Go-Seek, for gosh sakes."

I nodded and fell in beside him.

"It must have been a base in the old Jap war or something," said Hacker. "You can see the old runways through the grass."

The road curved ahead of us, and at the bend the jungle opened on scrub field. The two women stood by an old tin shack. The remains of two burned buildings lay in long grass. Hacker strode across the field and began to poke among these ruins. Corky Hacker and I stood watching him while Joan walked around the tin shack.

"You don't look so hot, Philip. Are you feeling all right?"

"Fine," I said.

"You probably smoked too much grass. If you're not used to it . . ." She left it at that and stared beyond the dark trees to where the sky was flushed. She looked tired and angry.

Joan came alongside. With my damaged throat I told her we were missing the sunrise. She looked at me severely. "Well, so what? It wasn't such a hot idea anyway. What I'd really like is a hot shower and some bacon and eggs. And then a long sleep."

"What I'd really like," said Corky Hacker, "is about ten Oreos and a glass of cold milk."

Turning to me, Joan said, "What are you talking in that funny voice for?"

"He probably smoked too much grass," said Corky.

Joan sniffed. "I daresay he did. They are so right when they say there's no fool like an old fool."

We stood watching Hacker as he walked around the derelict buildings. Corky Hacker suddenly cupped her hands and yelled at her husband. "Come on, Ted. I want to go now." In the pale morning light her face looked pinched and old as parchment.

"In a minute," called Hacker, who was now bent over. He seemed to be trying to wrest something from the earth. He straightened up and waved at us. "Come over here for a minute, will you!"

"Now what!" said Corky Hacker irritably.

The three of us trudged toward the stooping man. He had grasped a large metal ring and was trying to open a door into the ground. The heavy-looking iron door, rusted by weather and age, lay among the grass and weeds. Hacker again straightened up; he was red-faced and excited, breathing hard from his exertions. "I wonder what's underneath it."

"Well, who cares?" said Corky.

Hacker looked at her in dismay. "I care. Gosh, where's your sense of curiosity, Cork? Maybe there's something valuable down there. I'll bet it hasn't been opened in thirty or forty years."

"What a revolting thought!" said Joan.

Hacker winked at me. "Give me a hand, pal."

The two of us gripped the ring and pulled on the great door. Slowly it tore away from the earth, bearing with it tufts of grass and weeds. Once we had opened it a few inches, Hacker scrambled around and found purchase enough to push upward while I heaved. The door rose on loud complaining hinges, and revealed beneath were stone steps. A damp fetid smell filled our nostrils. Like children we peered cautiously down at stone untouched by daylight for years. The place had the grisly fascination of a tomb.

"Gosh," said Hacker, "I feel like Huckleberry Finn." He knelt to examine the darkness beyond the stone steps. "I wonder what it was used for? Maybe it was a bomb shelter or something?" He stood up and dusted the knees of his trousers.

Joan said, "I should have thought it was some kind of storage area."

"Yeah," said Hacker. "You're probably right. Say, do you know what it reminds me of?"

"What, Teddy?" asked Corky impatiently.

"It reminds me of Gramp Hacker's root cellar. On the farm Gramps had this old root cellar. There was a door on the side of the house that led down to it. That old root cellar is where my Gramps used to keep his swedes and spuds. I used to feed the spoiled ones to the hogs. Here pig, pig, pig, pig!" Seizing his nose between thumb and forefinger, Hacker produced some oinking sounds. Regrettably he was growing affable again.

"What do you say we have a look?"

"I'm not going down there, Teddy," Corky said. "It'll be so dirty."

"Oh come on, Cork. Don't be such a party poop. Papa Bear will look after you."

She took his hand, and the Hackers began to descend the stone stairs walking sideways. Joan shrugged and followed. "I suppose, while you're in foreign parts, you should enjoy all the sights. Come along, Philip."

"I'm right behind you, my precious one."

Crouching, I watched her disappear behind the others. Each was bent over, for there was not enough headroom to stand upright. "What a ghastly hole!" said Joan. "How far does it go?"

"Not far," said Hacker. "Too bad we haven't got a flashlight, but I don't think there's much to see anyway. It seems to be just an old tunnel. Probably somebody started something and didn't get around to finishing it. Here now! I can feel the end of it. Just dirt." I heard him laugh crazily. "Now I have you in my lair, little beauties."

"Teddy, don't, please," said Corky. "Don't be silly! Let's go back. I don't like it down here."

I saw Joan's trousered bottom coming through the gloom. She was backing out as I stood up and, placing my shoulder against the door, pushed mightily. It fell with a huge, satisfying thump, returning as if bidden to the place where it had lain undisturbed for so many years.

Corky Hacker began immediately to scream. Her muffled cries rose from the earth to the ears of the monster who was now busy dragging a large piece of timber (in memory, a kind of beam or joist) to lay across the door. I heard my wife say, "Thank God, Philip is still up there. Can you manage the door, darling? We'll all push from this side." Joan's voice had assumed that brittle quality affected by persons who are not quite used to panic, but who nevertheless are prepared to go to pieces if the occasion demands it.

There was now a good deal of coughing below decks. "Hurry, darling, please," called Joan. "It's really quite unpleasant down here."

"I should have thought so," I muttered, placing another piece of charred lumber over the grave.

"Pull the ring, Phil," cried Hacker. "Give her all you've

got, and we'll tackle her from this side. She should come. Corky, shut your goddamn mouth. You're getting on my nerves."

"Oh, Teddy, I hate it down here. Get me out!"

"I'll get you out if you shut your goddamn mouth."

"Philip! Please do hurry. There's not all that much bloody air down here."

They were now pounding on the door. "Philip!" yelled Joan. "Answer me, damn it! What are you doing up there?"

By the greatest good fortune, I discovered a large stone nearby and was able to roll that over the iron door.

"The darn thing won't budge," said Hacker. "Are you palling, pull? I mean pulling, pal?" He began to cough. I was now convinced that the door was secure. Stepping back, I listened for a final time to the bewildered and anguished pleas for assistance. They arose, if I may be permitted a literary touch, like the shrieks of the damned. I walked slowly away; the headache that had entered the right side of my brain had now settled over a larger area. I resolved never to smoke cannabis again.

Standing by the tin shack, I looked across the field at the ruined buildings and the jungle beyond. From where I stood, one could not for a moment imagine that beneath the grass three people were struggling for life. The sun had now risen and great shafts of light pierced the tops of the trees. It was time to be on my way.

As I walked down the road toward the highway, I gave some thought to explanations. It is, of course, not unheard of for people to disappear on holidays. I recalled Aunty Flo talking about Taffy Butterworth's wife, and of how she fell or was pushed from a fishing boat. They called it death by *misadventure*, a word that has always secretly thrilled me. Still, the disappearance of three persons would require a good story. There would be tiresome questions from the authorities, who would doubtless be suspicious. Yet, what could they do? Was it not necessary to have a body before laying charges? I regretted not knowing more about the wretched law.

I imagined some sort of inquiry at which I would be questioned by men wearing thick moustaches. It would be essential to maintain composure and answer with grave courtesy. In time they would allow me to return home. At the airport I would stand in the warm wind shaking hands with the chief of police. "We sincerely regret all this fuss we have put you through, Señor Bannister," the chief would say, brushing the dark hair from his eyes. "I trust this unfortunate business will not keep you from returning to Mexico. We have many charms to offer tourists."

"Not at all, my dear chief. I shall return."

"*Vaya con Dios*, Señor Bannister."

The following Sunday I would sit in my study after lunch and answer the scores of cards that arrived in my absence. With a glass of sherry and a tray of biscuits by my side, I would uncap my Waterman's fountain pen (a graduation gift from my aunts) and write to colleagues, former students, members of the board of governors, sympathetic strangers. *Thank you very much for your condolences. It has indeed been a very trying few weeks . . .*

It would probably look better if I passed up this year's cricket tour to England. Captain Hale would understand. *The poor fellow is still in mourning.* No longer would the boys speculate about my sexual proclivities; after all, I would now be a respectable middle-aged widower.

After the letters, there would be bells at dusk and the serenity of evensong. Later the Blakes would have me to dinner; Mrs. Neddy prepares a quite acceptable chicken paprika. With these agreeable images in mind, I continued down the road through the jungle, accompanied by bright green birds who darted from the trees to scold me, the saucy little beggars.

When I reached the Volkswagen buggy, however, I was soon dismayed. The key to the vehicle was not there! Damn Hacker must have put it into his pants pocket. What a pickle that put me in! I know nothing of motors and had no idea how to cross the wires or whatever it is you do to effect combustion in an automobile engine. And I didn't much fancy the idea of returning to that field to uncover my handiwork. Could I, for that matter, even lift the enormous door? And if so, could I face searching the pockets of a corpse? I sat dispirited behind the wheel, listening to the frightful squawking of the birds and contemplating my predicament.

To add to my dilemma, another Volkswagen buggy appeared on the horizon. What to do? Should I hide in the bushes? Or seek help? I was quickly discovering that murder is not the simple business many people make it out to be. I ran for the bushes, and was hiding behind a large clump of ferns when the vehicle passed. Then it slowed down, backed up, and stopped. "Hello there, my friend," said Mr. Yoshimodo. "You are having troubles?"

"Yes," I said, standing up. "I seem to have dropped my key."

"How very unfortunate," said the robot salesman. "Looking for a key in the jungle must be akin to looking for the needle in your famous haystack?"

"I'm afraid so," I said.

"Perhaps I can assist you," he said. "I am not unfamiliar with the mysteries of machinery." He was already peering under the hood. "I wish I had Sam Two here," he said. "He could fix this in what you people refer to as a jiffy."

"Sam Two?" I asked bleakly.

"Yes," he said. "A new line we are bringing out in the spring. He does wonderful work. He will soon replace the human hand, which, although a useful device, has its limitations." He smiled up at me. "And where is your wife and nice friends?"

"My wife and nice friends?" I croaked.

"Why, yes. I saw you all leave the hotel from my window. You are here no doubt to watch the rising sun? It is supposed to bring good fortune in the coming year. The rising sun is an important symbol to us Japanese. You may have noticed that it is on our flag."

How would it be, I wondered, if I were to murder Yoshimodo, too? Four instead of three? In for a penny, in for a pound, as the English put it. But how? No weapon was at hand and unarmed combat was out of the question. The Japanese are noted for their expertise in the martial arts.

Mr. Yoshimodo straightened up and wiped his useful devices with a polyester handkerchief. "It should go now, my friend. Oh look! The sun is coming up." He turned toward the great burning star and gravely bowed three times. "For luck." He winked. "And new growth areas in the world's economy." Then he jumped into his vehicle and sped away.

Twenty-Four

Today Mr. Gomez announced with regret that he was visiting me for the last time. Urgent business would keep him in Mexico City for the next several weeks, and he would unfortunately miss my trial. He was, however, sending along a nice Mr. Guitterez from his office and he would do very nicely. While he told me this, Mr. Gomez smiled and absently patted my arm. His thoughts seemed to be elsewhere. "Mr. Guitterez will be much better for you, Señor Bannister. I have acquainted him with all the particulars of your unfortunate situation, and at this very moment he is applying himself to the details. He will be in touch. Mr. Guitterez is an intelligent and energetic young man. Fresh out of the law academy. The very best type for a case like yours because, of course, he is eager to make a reputation for himself. And, as we used to say in the dormitory at The Gannymede, he will work like stink for you." Mr. Gomez laughed. "He is not a fat old goose like me."

While Mr. Gomez talked, old Miguel shuffled in and out of my cell in his bedroom slippers. Miguel was in high dudgeon. Not bothering to avert his ugly dead eye, he carried away the remnants of Miss Dodge's library. Watching him, Mr. Gomez whistled through his gold teeth. "Such a great many books, señor! I remember all the books we had to read at school. Robert Browning and Henry Longfellow. W. Shakespeare. 'You blocks, you stones, you worse than senseless things.' And, 'Out, out, damn sport!' Old Mr. Partridge! Do you remember him, señor? Perhaps he was before your time. How he used to make us memorize!"

Come said the wind to the leaves one day
Come over the meadow with me and play.

Mr. Gomez sighed heavily. "Literature! It is without a doubt a great consolation during adversity. But why is this unsightly viper removing your books?"

I explained that I no longer had money enough to retain Miguel and his various services. Listening, Mr. Gomez shook his head knowingly. "Money is so often at the root of distress. Is that not so? I believe it to be true. But you cannot expect much loyalty from these local Indians, señor. They are a temperamental bunch and given to superstition. Serpent worship and corn gods and all the rest of it. You are probably better off without him." He smiled. "But allow me to show you something splendid. It may cheer your heart to see it."

From his billfold he brought forth a snapshot and handed it to me. "Fernando," he said, "has made the Junior School third team. Another Ralph Hotchkiss in the making, eh!" He laughed. "I am having a joke, of course. But is this not an occasion for rejoicing?" My eyes watered as I stared at the photograph of the small, fat Mexican boy in a Gannymede hockey uniform. Mr. Gomez regarded me gravely and, shaking out a large white handkerchief, blew his nose. "Ah, you are affected, señor. Is it not so when all members of the Gannymede family see a young one in the old school colours? But forgive me, dear sir. I had no desire to upset you. I can see now that you are a sensitive man. And you are a long way from the old school, are you not?"

I handed back the photograph and we shook hands. A scowling Miguel had removed the last of the books, and my little cell seemed particularly bereft.

Miguel had left the door open and so, looking down at his smart Italian shoes, Mr. Gomez stepped into the corridor. "Well, *adiós*, Señor Bannister," he said, closing the door. "I am sure that we will meet again under happier circumstances. Perhaps a Founders' Day weekend? I try to attend now and again." Once more he offered me a plump hand and we shook through the bars. "Please take heart, señor," said Mr. Gomez. "It is always darkness before the dawn. And always in times of misery I remember what Snuffy Hobbs used to say. You must remember Snuffy? Such a great coach and a good man, too. Very fair. When he gave you the old rattan, he always provided the why and the wherefore. Not like some of the others. Anyway, before a game Snuffy always called his players over to the bench for a chat. I used to lean by the boards and listen. And always Snuffy would say, "Shoot low on the stick side, boys!" Mr. Gomez laughed and his teeth gleamed in the sickly yellow light. "So, Señor Bannister. Do not forget, eh! Shoot low on the stick side!"

Twenty-Five

Ninety-nine years seems a very long time, and I said as much to the presiding officer of the court, a gloomy, handsome man who cannot yet have seen his fortieth birthday. When you reach your middle years, you discover with both alarm and chagrin that the people who minister unto you—the urologist with his cystoscope, the dentist with his air drill, the judge with his precepts—are all younger. I had expected someone older and more sympathetic, but the man who handed down this grievous sentence looked like a matinee idol with his sleek dark hair and sallow good looks.

But that was months ago; water over the bridge, as Mr. Gomez used to say. And prison life is not so different from my days in the boarding school. At six o'clock in the morning I am awakened by the bells, and sixteen hours later the bells ring for "lights out." In between there are bells for dressing, eating, and games. Soccer and baseball are popular with my fellow prisoners, but I have approached the chief warder with the idea of introducing cricket. When I explained the rules to him, he sounded intrigued and thought it might be just the game for long-term inmates.

All in all, there is a satisfying order to the diurnal routine here. I am not saying it is for everyone; I am perhaps a special case and I am thankful for my long years at The

Gannymede. They have certainly held me in good stead for this kind of life. I am also more fortunate than others because I have a little money coming in from my pension fund. Four times a year Tubby Barrett in the bursar's office sends me a small cheque. This allows me to bribe the guards for little favours. They are avaricious young fellows who are saving for motor scooters and colour television sets. How I miss old Miguel with his simple peasant greed! With my pension cheque I am also able to buy Ivory Snow and aspirin and books. I have even opened a small account with a bookstore in Mexico City and I am now collecting the 1904 editions of Bulwer-Lytton's novels. It's amazing how his work has held up over the years in Mexico; only the other day I received a well-thumbed copy of *The Lady of Lyons*.

My Spanish is coming along nicely and three afternoons a week I teach English as a second language to other murderers and thieves. By and large I have to say that I find them more attentive than Canadian schoolboys. In return for this service the chief warder invites me to his cottage on Sunday nights for a game of draughts and a glass of tequila. He also allows me to take his dog for a stroll each evening in the compound. I enjoy this outing and have grown fond of the animal, a brown pug whose tail curls upward to expose a large convoluted anus. I call him Bullseye. He looks surly but is really only shy and quite affectionate. When he squats to apply himself in the shadows of the evening, Bullseye gazes up at me with mournful, embarrassed eyes. Yet his grin of exertion serves to remind me that life is also humble creaturely function.

• • •

Today's post brought a letter from Neddy Blake. My old enemy Milo Murdoch is dead. Heart attack over the noon meal in Bung Hall, poor fellow. And so Milo, an exemplary citizen, if somewhat sly and overly ambitious, lies in his grave while I, a killer, play draughts with my jailer. Surely such developments are beyond comprehension. Neddy also tells me that Bea Corcoran is planning a trip to Mexico next summer and would like to look me up. Tomorrow I intend to write to Bea advising her against travel.